T0013900

Loved and Missed

Loved and Missed

SUSIE BOYT

nyrb **New York Review Books** New York

This is a New York Review Book

published by The New York Review of Books

207 East 32nd Street, New York, NY 10016

www.nyrb.com

For Mary and Cecilia

Copyright © 2021 by Susie Boyt
All rights reserved.

LIBRARY OF CONGRESS CATALOGING-IN-PUBLICATION DATA
Names: Boyt, Susie, 1969– author.
Title: Loved and missed / by Susie Boyt.
Description: New York : New York Review Books, [2023]
Identifiers: LCCN 2022059091 (print) | LCCN 2022059092 (ebook) |
  ISBN 9781681377810 (paperback) | ISBN 9781681377827 (ebook)
Subjects: LCSH: Mothers and daughters—Fiction. | Grandparent and
  child—Fiction. | Drug addiction—Fiction. | LCGFT: Novels.
Classification: LCC PR6052.099 L683 2023 (print) | LCC PR6052.
  099 (ebook) | DDC 823/.914—dc23/eng/20221220
LC record available at https://lccn.loc.gov/2022059091
LC ebook record available at https://lccn.loc.gov/2022059092

ISBN 978-1-68137-781-0
Available as an electronic book; ISBN 978-1-68137-782-7

Printed in the United States of America on acid-free paper.

10 9 8 7 6 5 4 3 2

I forgive you Maria
Things can never be the same,
But I forgive you Maria
Though I think you were to blame,
I forgive you Maria,
I can never forget,
But I forgive you, Maria
Kindly remember that.

STEVIE SMITH

ONE

I had a few old ghosts in the evening, a solemn deposition in coats and scarves. I still thought of them as the girls – Christine, Sarah, Fran – we were a tight four at one point, taking the piss out of each other religiously, confiding at the bus stop in our Courtelle V-necks, high-spirited, insane for mascara, a bit valiant, desperate to trespass.

Christine reigned over us: glossy in her looks and personality. She was Snow White-ish in appearance, only more turbulent in character – sharp, smart, clever, quite clever – and you were a bit amazed when she liked you, alarmed even as you were buoyed by the flattery. I once used the word 'traitorous' in front of her, which isn't much of a word and I regretted it for weeks although it *is* in the dictionary. She has softened slightly. The sarcasm's gone out of her. Thirty years ago her husband Luke left her with two small children, surprising everyone, then nine years later he wrote a letter on blue paper asking to come home, just like that.

I hadn't seen her for a long time, but she rang me and we met to discuss it. It was cold and windy but she wanted to walk, she felt the rhythm of walking would help things fall into place, that and the bracing light. I brought an exercise book and two sharp pencils and we sat on a broken-slatted bench in Finsbury Park, the edges of our knees lightly touching. Christine had dressed for the occasion: wine-coloured Spanish boots and a good-looking raincoat that flapped in the wind, and we made two columns, one for yes and one for no. I didn't contribute much. I wasn't sure how to frame myself. But I nodded loyally at intervals, took pains not to inflame any outrage. We had no trouble filling the no column – he put raw onion in the salad, undid his filthy bike onto the kitchen table, and that wasn't the half of it – still, she took him back. A mistake, I thought, when the trust was gone. If he had done it once, she said, well, three times that she knew of. He was the kind of man for whom everyday life involved a series of evasions; secrets and hiding were second nature to him, subtle vanishing acts. He valued his privacy so much he didn't even like being asked how he was.

'D'you ever run into him, round and about?' she said.

'No.' I shook my head.

He told me once he had a horror of unlived life, which I could only translate as a disdain for the ties of home. But he had this star-tling way of making you less uninteresting to yourself, at the end of the day, or in the morning. And he was moved by her generosity of spirit, felt lucky and grateful to be allowed back in and he settled himself, spent much of his free time plotting things to make her and the boys happy. She was a painter and now the children had left home she could paint all day long, all night sometimes, distrait in paint-spattered navy French overalls. Quite a good painter, also, although I worried her pictures had a forced intensity. That it wasn't about anything. She had exhibitions every three years or so. Perhaps that's spiteful of me. I could be spiteful at times.

Sarah and Fran were still best friends and lived in adjacent streets. Fran worked hard at a children's publishers; she was a self-contained, conscientious and precise person. I've never known her not on her own. She was writing a novel herself now – about her parents' sex life, apparently – but I can't say more, she said, as though I wasn't mature enough for the material. Sarah was softer, messy-looking, generous. She lived with Geoff these days – he was a bit booming and hearty for my taste, an amazing cook, although didn't he go on about it – and she had recently left teaching. She wanted a second act, she said, and she had opened a tiny shop in the corner of an antiques market, eight foot by eight foot with a deadly metal spiral staircase and an even smaller upper floor. She sold old clothes there: Victorian white nighties, beaded cardigans, flower-strewn 1930s silk and crêpe dresses and lace curtains that she sometimes made up into Edwardian-style wedding attire. It was a romantic setting for her, she thought, casting a pale golden light over things compared to the grey shadows of the blackboard, which flattered no one at all. But she spent every second of her free time mending now, instead of marking, which was heroic and feminine yes, but was it progress? I was not convinced.

I was not sure what they would say about me. Tall, chestnut-haired, despairing? Would they claim in order to be brave I've had to coarsen myself?

We sat in my little sitting room, having portioned ourselves out on the sea-green armchairs and the old blue sofa, half whispering as Lily slept in the next room. When no one spoke you could catch her inward breaths. I loved to listen to her sleeping because it sounded as though she was inhaling life. They all wanted to know about Eleanor; at least they asked, but I never knew what to say. 'She's the same', I tried that sometimes, or a wry 'Oh, you know', but it was hard to get the right tone. A few years back I made a mistake and told their eager ears, 'She's stable', meaning I wasn't aware of any recent deterioration, which isn't quite what 'stable' means. At first they took it as a declaration of improvement, offering wide pleading smiles, misty-eyed congratulation, but no one picked me up on it when they realised. Sometimes I worried they would find my sadness insufficient or think my courage had failed me. I could always tell when there was something in the air: uneasiness, judgement, an odd sort of lawless pressure that made me harden.

There was an idea that having Lily compensated me in various ways for losing Eleanor. When I listened to her processing her day in comical murmurs through the baby monitor while I sat marking at the kitchen table, there *was* a sort of bright perfection to the two of us. I always smiled as the wearier she grew the more international her self-talk sounded. But if Lily thought it was her job to patch me up, I would have doubly failed.

'Thank God you've got your teaching,' Christine said, Sarah said, Fran. That well-known panacea! (It was word for word what they'd said to me when we last met a couple of years ago.) I passed round glasses of straw-coloured wine. My old school friends already had cushions for their backs and glasses of water and green olives stuffed with almond slivers or bright tongues of red pepper from a jar. The cornflower-blue cardigan I was knitting for Lily lay arms outstretched on the side of my chair. In their company, I noticed, I tried to be extra nurturing in my atmosphere. Perhaps I needed them to know that Eleanor was once in possession of valuable things she squandered, which she chose to squander. That is one of the difficult things about personality – in order to convey it effectively there is always that faint smell of acting that muddies things. I needed them to see me in a merciful light. Perhaps it was just that I was very tired.

'I saw something, in the week, but I didn't know whether to mention it,' Christine was saying.

'Oh?'

'I mean it was nothing much, but – oh, I don't know. Actually, forget it. I shouldn't have said anything.'

That was the kind of thing I couldn't stand.

'You'll have to tell her now,' Sarah murmured.

'Is it something bad?

'No-oh. Not really, not bad, not really bad.'

'Can you say?'

'Well I was walking back from Sainsbury's and I passed the Tube and you know the bit outside where there are often street people drinking, tramps and things, and there was a little group sitting bundled up by the entrance, with sleeping bags and stuff laid all around, bottles and packets, blankets, milk, cigarettes, there was a box of cereal I think and there was a little sign asking for money and one of them had a great big dog, and one of them had a guitar and one of them, one of them was Eleanor.'

'Oh.'

'I mean they looked quite merry. *In their way.*'

'You make it sound almost – what's the word – *picaresque.*' I thought of a bag lady I often said hello to, who cuddled her wild possessions closely to her as though they were family.

'It wasn't quite like that.'

'No, no. I was, it was, a joke.'

'What was difficult was I hadn't seen her for a few years, and the change in her, and when I saw her I just didn't know how—'

'You got a shock. Of course. It's understandable.' I tried to sound mild, but it was a strain.

'I was rather shocked, yes. It seemed almost as though—'

I had a horror of people using figurative language at these junctures. 'She had the look of a beautiful garment, half ruined by poor laundering.' 'Her face a map of ruined days' or whatever. 'Ruined choirs', I couldn't bear that. Something cobbled together from a reject Shakespeare sonnet. Eleanor had always been considered quite beautiful and it was a bit much the way people were thrilled it might no longer hold true. Had they held it against us in the past? (She did have that aloofness very good looks can bring.) Once, one of them said she looked 'ripe for pneumonia', as though it were a sort of *reference*. I knew I mustn't mind these things.

'I'm sorry,' I said simply. 'I do apologise. It must have been—'

'No, no, no,' she said, 'I didn't mean for a second that *you* should have to—'

'It's OK,' I said. 'It's fine. It's just something . . . ' I rocked to and fro in my chair and I had tears, but they weren't particularly hot. There was something sensible about them.

'Oh Ruth! I've made you cry. Oh how awful!'

'Please don't worry – it's just, it's just chemistry.' I blotted my eyes on my knuckles.

'I don't know if this was right or wrong,' Christine was saying, 'but I went over and gave her a kiss on the forehead, and she wasn't smelly or dirty like the others or anything, but her hair is quite thin now, you know, stringy and rather sad-looking, and you could see the pink of her scalp, sort of raw pink, and forgive me if this was very bad, but I gave her a tenner. I just couldn't not.'

That knocked me out a little bit. 'Thank you,' I said, sincerely grateful. I didn't know I could still feel grateful, exactly; it felt so old-school, unnatural almost, lacking in stealth and belonging to a part of my life that was gone. When Eleanor had chickenpox, I dipped a cotton bud in the bottle of calamine lotion, painted small pink petals round the spots, joining up the dots with leaves and filigree vines across her feverish body, watching the flowers dry to chalky white. That was a sincere time. I closed my eyes for a second. I didn't care about the money but I minded that her hair, which surely in its way was innocent, had been so roundly condemned.

There was a lot of pressure in the room suddenly. It was clear that no one wanted to say or feel anything without my tacit permission. My friends knew I could be critical. It was intimate almost to the point of suffocation, that little room throbbing with stretched feminine nerves and my old school friends sitting there bathing in fine fellow feeling or trying to, trying not to, it was so hard to tell. Sarah had a rogue tear on her cheek and she swiped it away with her thumbnail, leaving a brief crimson scratch. I didn't want things like that.

It was a blank October day, uncertain. The sun was low and shapeless now. The light began to fail entirely and I noticed the lustre of the street lamps as they came on, one by one. Shame. Regret. Sorrow. The following day the clocks were going back. The bright sprint to Christmas. I didn't know how I was going to keep buoyant. The exorbitant levels of pride my life seemed to demand. That, or absolutely none at all. In the street outside I watched two little girls loop and tie a length of rope round a lamp post and one of them skipped in and out as the other turned it rhythmically. *'Rosy apple lemon tart, tell me the name of your sweetheart. A, B, C, D . . . '* There was sudden shouting, the slam of a car door, and I watched a young woman in a short black dress running down the street, shrieking with laughter, her white shoulder bag flapping.

'What can we do?' Sarah pleaded. 'What can we do for you, Ruth?'

I couldn't see their needing to help me was my problem, quite. I had fantasies of wild insurrection, but I just smiled.

At that exact point Lily stumbled into the room, heroic in blue and white night clothes, eyelids pink and crusted yellow at the corners from sleep, curls flattened and crushed. She blinked and took in the women as though it were a dream almost, and she put her hand over her eyes – it was a faintly Garbo-like move, I thought, a stunning silent-movie gesture – and she bundled herself onto my lap, so many long limbs it seemed she had, six or nine, attaching herself to me as though she were a koala and I a tree, not that exactly, but there was a declaration in her movements that I was, my body was, her home, her natural habitat. If you had told me then she had come out of me, I would have believed you.

I sat for a second, completely still in the face of what struck me as tremendous loyalty. I was certain the women assembled were jealous of me suddenly, in a way that would not have been conceivable even two minutes before. For a moment my life hardly felt smashed up at all.

They let themselves out and I sat for a time in semi-darkness, Lily still laid out across me, the swell of gratitude solid in my body and I closed my eyes, peaceful in the hot calm coming from her arms and legs, and started to daydream. I felt traces of a Christmas from a few years ago that was very sharp-edged. The goals have changed, though, the hopes have adjusted themselves down realistically, and that strange day seemed like an old photograph discarded because you looked sour or plain or deranged but, of course, finding it again in a packet of old letters a few years later you'd give quite a bit to be like that now.

Eleanor hadn't wanted to see me over the festive season – three years ago this was, near enough – but she agreed to meet for a walk on the afternoon of December 25th. I said, 'How about a picnic?' and she didn't tell me to get lost so I suggested Regent's Park, somewhere with a sense of occasion; sometimes you needed swans and a lake and a bandstand. 'Pick you up at one-ish and we can zoom over there?' but she told me to meet her instead at a modest strip of grass next to a main road, a few minutes from where she lived in Holloway.

It was a greyish day, stubbornly unremarkable, with a grey careless light hanging over everything. It was ordinary for me waking alone on Christmas morning, but in a small way, if I was truthful, it hurt my pride. The park had one or two sprawling dusty bushes and three wooden benches, one of which served the adjacent bus stop, but it was more of a glorified traffic island, treeless in the main and outlawed-looking. Certainly somewhere to avoid at night. When I arrived she was sitting on the bus stop bench with Ben, underdressed against the weather, her long bright hair splayed across her shoulders in the dreary light almost like thin tinsel strips, the pair looking about them with an air of expectation, as though no one had told them buses did not exist on Christmas Day. Ben smiled; he had a light, gruff optimism about him that felt close to festive. He stood and kissed me hello, affectionate towards the universe. It was the third time we had met, and his greeting made me feel she could scarcely have poisoned him against me.

'Merry Christmas!' I called out, and they both smiled as though I had paid them far-fetched compliments. I motioned that we might venture inside the park – why not, it was Christmas after all – rather than stick to the bench by the street. They followed me in but Eleanor settled on another bench right away, as though she were rather elderly or her joints had become stiff or painful.

'We haven't got long,' she said.

'All right, love.' She was so pale.

I had the sense I was performing something or someone as I fished the flask of coffee from my bag and poured it out into the three white enamel cups with blue rims, and milk – hot milk – from a smaller container. I felt foolish as I handed Eleanor her stocking, attention-seeking, like a flasher almost. 'Mum!' she yelped, but she sounded pleased. She didn't open it, but held it close to her like a small pet in her arms. I could feel the red crêpe paper on the parcels softening against the heat of her body; a ring of silver string slipped to the ground. For Ben I had bought an old Black Watch tartan scarf from Sarah's shop – anyone would like that, wouldn't they? It had some heft to it, a gent's scarf, dignified. I'd have liked it myself. He opened the present right away, tore it open. He looked delighted. It was surprisingly elegant, and he wrapped the scarf round his neck and began murmuring, happy, bashful, dopey: 'It's too good for me.'

'Nonsense!' I said. 'Don't be silly!' We all laughed, but the laughter sounded dangerous.

I got my courage up and spread three red-checked dishcloths on the old bench, placed some gold paper plates in a triangle, unwrapped the turkey sandwiches I had made, the meat half white, half brown, still warm, the butter glistening. I had chestnut stuffing wrapped in foil and I crumbled it over the meat, smeared on cranberry sauce from a coffee jar with the back of a spoon. I set down a paper cup full of sprouts on the bench. My hand was shaking. 'Christmas vitamins,' I mumbled wryly, but they looked slightly fraudulent, as though they might have been pretending. I had three small bottles of Coke, the curvaceous ones – I've always had a horror of things that were too wholesome – and red-and-white-striped straws in case anyone wanted that. I had a box of six crackers with robins on them in a carrier and I laid two next to each plate. I had forgotten the paper napkins with the holly sprigs. I propped a tall red candle in an eggcup and lit the wick, sheltering it with the curve of my hand, the flame hot on my fingers until the fucking wind blew it out. No one said anything. I was very aware of my feet pressed into the hard ground suddenly, of thin grey air, emptiness underfoot and overhead, uneven breaths. I numbed myself deliberately. We all acted as though it was completely normal, as though we were having Christmas dinner on the day the world had ended.

It started to rain lightly and the strained occasion began to wilt. I thought of the table in my flat, the soft chairs, the hypnotising coal fire. Ben had some food but Eleanor wasn't going to, I could tell. Her appetite was erratic, like a lot of young girls intent on cancelling themselves. She thought she had already been extravagant in coming out. A snatch of carol played at the back of my throat, six brisk notes sharply rising. I couldn't think of the words. Oh. *Let nothing you dismay.*

Ben put down his sandwich – three crescent-shaped bite marks. He had used up all his politeness and there was only mounting impatience now, fledgling nervy hostility rising, darting eye movements exchanged between them, flashes of contempt. Once or twice it seemed as though Eleanor was on the verge of telling me some caustic home truth, scythe-mouth narrowing against me. I got out a small wooden box of Turkish delight (why did I?), lifted the balsa-wood lid with the apple-green lettering, unfolding the silver paper, which was powdery on its underside, like the wrapping in a packet of cigarettes. Beneath the foil a slip of white waxed paper and underneath softly coloured order and plenty, rose and lemon squares tightly packed, eleven perfect scented rows, pink yellow pink yellow, beneath a thin dusting of icing sugar mixed with cornflour, texture of dry snow. They both shook their heads, of course they did. I couldn't think of anything else then, my bag of tricks completely empty. The moment grew increasingly fragile. Around me there was little that was green, the elderly grass muddied and littered with packets and dog-ends and cans; what plants there were looked mangled and bereft. I was smiling all the while, just gently, but in my heart I was thinking this might be the saddest occasion of my life.

I have known greater sadness since, of course, and in my devious memory the forlorn gathering, viewed from some acute angles, did shimmer with a certain jagged grace, like a classic album cover or something, a still from a well-loved bleak European film: the wary older woman, with odd folkloric determination, rigging up thin Christmas cheer. The cauterising silhouettes of bare trees – all that. I knew I was stodgy with intentions and conventions; the beautiful frail mysterious pair – islands of remoteness – resisting, indulging, shunning, ignoring, enduring. Of course, memories always changed a little each time you retrieved them; small and big adjustments to the proportions were necessary as they served your purpose or you served theirs. But it was such a hard day.

We said our goodbyes. They were glazed with boredom now. Eleanor's head swivelled round when I made to kiss her so all I got was a mouthful of hair. If people asked me with not enough or too much tact, 'Did you get a chance to cross over with Eleanor during the break at all?' at least I would be able to answer truthfully that—

'Mum?'

'Yes?'

'Tell you something?'

'Please.'

'Gonna have a child,' she said. 'A little girl.'

I saw a sudden brightness in her eyes and then I flung my arms around her. 'What do you need?'

TWO

On the morning of the christening I took the Sickert in a Sainsbury's carrier to a man off Bond Street. We stood facing each other while I muttered something formal and incoherent. We were in a darkish Italian café, three quarters empty. Twelve shiny lozenge-shaped rosewood-effect tables, not much wider than ironing boards and Elvis droning on and on about missed opportunities.

I was nervous; I felt shipwrecked almost, ship-racked. He took the brown paper from the painting, narrowed his mouth, dipped his shoulders. He was organising himself for disappointment, I could see. I stored it up, his little insincere routine, thought it might come in useful later. The man was wiry and weak-chested with a stale Dickensian pallor. Nicotine stains on all ten of his fingers. Wild of hair.

I sat roughly, bashing my elbow on the side of the chair and they brought us small coffees, one black, one white. There was grease on the saucers, the smell of burnt toast, and a large waitress in her pink overall was preparing for lunchtime, slicing beefsteak tomatoes with a serrated knife, undoing a yellow lettuce leaf by leaf.

'It's not a *great* picture,' he said. 'A sketch.'

The ancient-looking painting of a sparrow-like figure on stage in white organdie, flanked by red curtains, one arm raised in the direction of the gallery, was the best thing I had.

'*Oh?*' I heard a certain sharp thinness in my voice. I gulped down some coffee. I was so exhausted, I very nearly didn't care. The way it had been given to me had been a bit terrible – one of those things you have to try to forget even as it is happening.

'It is what it is,' the man answered.

What happened next was that he took a small padded envelope from a black holdall at his feet and I carried it to the café toilets, unzipped it and counted the money into the little hand basin. Four hundred brand-new ten-pound notes in four bundles, strong-smelling, crisp-edged: the Queen on one side, Florence Nightingale on the other, doing their thing. I thought of the three of us sitting on a park bench together, Her Majesty clasping a glossy sceptre and a little yapping corgi, Florence benign and powerful, a black ribbon at her throat, me lulling the baby in her christening robe. Or her little footed babygro or whatever they wore for christenings now, those with no religious faith to speak of who were undergoing hard times and could not or would not cope.

I stuffed the notes back into the envelope, shoved it inside my jumper, buttoned my coat, rinsed the smell of money from my hands. My face in the mirror looked weary, suspicious. My imagination had had so much to do lately, apart from anything else.

I emerged from the ladies', barked, 'All right then' at the man's unappetising smile and walked briskly away from everything. It was early November on Oxford Street, the air mildish with a light wind, the shops threatening Christmas. My state of mind was pretty good.

The bus was crowded and I had to stand until Euston, the money lodged next to my skin, warming my ribs. I had looked up the church in a book of London churches in the school library. I did two and a half days a week now, twenty hours. 'You only want to teach the clever girls,' Mrs Hadley said. 'Well I'm afraid one can't insist on roast beef *every* day.' Such an odd thing to say.

The triple-arched entrance contains mosaic decoration in the arches, and opens onto a broad passage through the body of the building that emerges under a deep west gallery into the aisleless nave.

Outside the church there wasn't anyone about, and when I poked my head round the carved wooden doors there were only three or four straggling worshippers. A schoolgirl on her knees in green-and-white-checked uniform, twin French plaits snaking down her back, that was poignant.

And then I heard them, a little throng of merry revellers, led by Eleanor and Ben, wandering up the other side of the street. They had been wetting the baby's head evidently and had a rogue processional Pied Piper air. Ben was carrying Lily, who was smiling. He wore suit trousers, but they were ancient, miles too big, and he billowed round his edges, mad and comic, Chaplinesque. Eleanor wheeled the pram behind them. She had on a straggly black skirt and an enormous holey charcoal V-neck, long sleeves breaking into thick crinkled strands. Her fair hair was scraped back severely like a dancer, thin hoop earrings, her wide and generous mouth from a distance like a mirage. One or two of their party were clutching bottles of beer. One had a guitar. There were three cans in the navy pram with the silver trim I had bought them.

Eleanor saw me and waved hazily as though she was much further away than she was. She took Lily from Ben, crossed the road and came up to me.

'Here you go.' She plonked her in my arms, turning away.

'Hello precious,' I mouthed to the child, kissing the kink in her silky hair. Lily was her usual irreproachable self. She wasn't dressed up in the slightest, but you could tell she sensed it was a special day and she was wide awake and in adventurous mood, eyes smiling at me curiously. Maybe white terry towelling for a christening was chic? Seaside-ish. Freshly baked. A dressed-up baby, a formal tot bound in dusty lace like a child bride was an appalling idea, possibly. She was clean.

I couldn't look at Eleanor closely, not when we were celebrating. I sometimes thought what I minded most was that all the kindness had gone from her face. The way she had profaned her body.

My eyes safely hovering a few inches above her head, I congratulated her with the biggest smile I had on me. I hoped I wouldn't offend her with approximated cheer. I squinted at Ben chatting to the men with the beer bottles. He carried it well, his brand of cavern-faced mania, in part because he was tall and serious and he already had the atmosphere of distractedness clever people often have. Either that or his warm-hearted confusion was oddly endearing. He brought more of himself to this life, I felt, than she did. I didn't expect very much from him, perhaps that was all it was. And of course it wasn't nothing that they were all more or less on time and Lily looked all right and he'd put on a white shirt with a collar and Eleanor's smile had a certain high wattage, although she looked half crazed, scratching at her neck repeatedly, hollow-cheeked, hard red-rimmed eyes. They were doing their best.

Jean Reynolds from school had offered to be my date. We'd been working side by side for almost two decades and were quite friendly these days, after several years of polite fascination. On both sides, I liked to think.

'I'd do you proud,' she said. 'I have hats, I have brooches.'

I laughed. 'I'm sure you do, but ...'

'You'd rather keep things simple?'

'If you don't mind.'

I made myself give Eleanor a hug, feeding my free arm round her, imprecisely. 'Congratulations. You're a genius!' I nodded towards the babe, which was a masterpiece. Lily launched herself into the cuddle like the filling in a sandwich.

The priest appeared, calling out bright hullo hullos. He wore his good looks with a certain luxurious amusement. He was tall, strong-set, dark-eyed, effusive. Perhaps he had been told to make a fuss of me. He said it was a *pleasure* to meet me and that Ben and Eleanor had told him what a *wonderful* support I was and how they couldn't have done it without me.

'It's my absolute *pleasure*.' I was drunk on him suddenly. Usually I could only endure sympathy that was lightly done – it was such a hard thing to convey – but his tone was just right. His church was an inclusive church and that didn't just mean welcoming all-comers, he said, because that was, that was a given, but providing support in the community and hot dinners and baby clothes and a soup-and-sonatas drop-in for the elderly parishioners on Mondays. He wanted to get a community fridge project off the ground – they were everywhere in New Zealand – that was his next *initiative*.

'That sounds really *interesting*,' I heard myself say. His dark curly hair sprang forward suddenly, releasing itself over his ears and forehead, and sheepishly he batted it away. He was so ani-mated. I appreciated the fact that there was nothing gaunt about him. He made me think of Oscar Wilde.

'Music and movement for the under fives on Tuesday after-noons,' he continued with a flourish. 'Single-dad Thursdays.' He laughed and coloured slightly. For half a second I thought he was going to confide something lavish to me – 'You know I've one or two myself, off the record' – but no such luck.

He thanked me for coming. 'You've got your hands full, I imagine. Can't be easy.'

'Well ...' Luckily Lily beamed at that exact moment in my arms and she was very contagious and I said to the priest, 'Of course *she* makes it easy.'

He nodded. 'She looks to have a very good nature.'

Outside the church some ragged clumps of marigolds grew in grey slatted wooden tubs dotted with cigarette butts and scraps of confetti. A street sweeper was rounding up piles of withered leaves. 'Shall we?' The priest took my arm, supporting the point of my elbow with his fingertips. Was he this courtly with all his people? I quite liked being treated like the mother of the bride. We all went into the church, took our seats at the front, first three rows of stark brown pews were fullish, perhaps thirty of us altogether. There was a strong odour of incense mixed with wax polish and disinfectant; a wave of artificial vanilla from my neighbour's violent scent. Someone put a tape on – 'God only knows what I'd be without you'. I sat down with Lily propped up on my lap, my arm firm across her warm middle, jiggling my knee up and down rhythmically. An older woman passed us a fine white shawl edged in satin. She was something to do with the church possibly. I thanked her, sniffed it discreetly; it smelled only of wool and soap flakes and although it wasn't new, it was lightly matted, it looked clean, so I gathered it into a little dress shape over Lily's babygro – it was cool in the church – and she began cuddling it so that was good. I patted the envelope of money – paper armour against my heart – and felt the swell of anxious calculations. You need to get your courage up, I mouthed the words. Concentrate.

Lily was light in my arms, too light possibly, for seven months; the heaviest thing about her was her nappy. I nipped up the back of the church and used a pew as a changing table, laid out a folding mat on some kneelers with basic tapestry of London landmarks: the Post Office Tower, Big Ben, Marble Arch. When I finished I splashed a few drops of holy water on her belly button for a sort of joke. I wasn't religious any more. I didn't suppose Lily was. Eleanor certainly wasn't. Lily chuckled as I sprinkled her. She wore a good, strong, past-caring look as I did up the silver poppers on her suit. Her facial expressions sometimes reminded me of an elderly Jewish comedian. I winked at her. She very nearly returned the gesture.

I had to be quite stoic when I was with Eleanor – if I looked in any way aggrieved, she would not speak – but I forgot in my panic that seeing me spritz myself all over with false brightness disgusted her a little bit also. I was not in love with it myself. She hated anything resembling dishonesty or performance, but if I faced her truthfully she would probably never see me again. What did she think courage was? She could be so exacting; but it was a day for generosity, or if not generosity then painstaking kindness, and if I couldn't run to that then a hazy sort of last-ditch myopic indulgence. I despised these sorts of downwards adjustments which made me feel miserly. An uncouth relation in a Jane Austen. Something like that, anyway.

It was five to twelve. The tentative rain was gathering strength, chipping against the high windows, thickening the congregation. A man about my age, mid fifties, settled himself in front of me, propping up a young red-haired woman whose eyes kept closing. Every now and then he prodded her affectionately in the ribs with his elbow or his rolled-up *Standard* and she'd come to and smile and switch herself on for a minute brightly and giggle and seem to be winning at things, and then she would soften herself, her shoulders and her features would sag and dim and she'd slump forward again, as though a fascinating scene was playing out in her lap. It wasn't dramatic, all very light and soft and casual, these small flashes of animation, but her red hair was wild against the man's sharp navy blazer, some of her corkscrew curls like telephone cable coming out of her head at right angles. Her freckles had a life of their own.

Suddenly she turned her head and stared at me hard.

'Hello, miss,' she said. 'It's me, miss. Sheila O'Neil,' and then I realised. Taught her English in the fourth and fifth years, she was in Eleanor's form, she'd been an amazing gymnast, famous for doing strings of cartwheels all round the playground, more of a firework than a girl I remembered thinking: blazing colour-bursts and fizzing bright light and long freckled legs where her head should be, mad bouncing curls, livelier than life. She'd left at sixteen. I tried to talk her out of it. 'I've got to get on with my future, miss.'

'Sheila.' I crisped myself. 'How lovely to see you!'

'Thanks, miss. You too. You think it's no smoking?'

'Oh I do, yes. You know what churches are like.'

'Yeah, boring.'

The priest sidled back over to us. I stood up. 'Your daughter wonders if you would consider being Lily's godmother, whether that might be something you'd . . . ?' He brought the palms of his hands together apologetically.

Whoever heard of a grandmother being godmother? But it didn't matter, and I had heard of aunts and uncles being godparents; big sisters and cousins and so on, so I said, 'Thanks. I'd love to.' The priest nodded in Eleanor's direction. He looked relieved.

'And if there's a reading you'd like to do, or a poem, or even if you've a mind to, a song perhaps . . .' He was embarrassed now; he let it show with a small mock wince as if the blame was all his and he really ought to know better. I was grateful it didn't seem to occur to him to humiliate me. 'Short notice, I know,' he cringed. He was so polite he almost made you feel you were the priest. *Bless you my son!*

The other godparent hadn't materialised – Ben nipped out to telephone him from the phone box by the big Sainsbury's. There didn't seem to be anyone from Ben's family either. He had at least a mother and a brother to his name, a sister in Edinburgh who was doing *tough love*, but not today.

Father Pat was pacing up and down looking at his watch for answers. That was the thing, you started off hell-bent on a rescue mission and before you knew it you got mashed up.

I whispered to Eleanor, 'Who's the most sensible person here?'

'What's that supposed to mean?'

'Sorry, the kindest then, that was what I was thinking, what I meant to say. Sorry.'

She pointed to Sheila.

'*Well* . . .' I said. Sheila was not currently conscious. 'Well . . . I'm not entirely—'

Eleanor's grey-blue eyes sent out flares of contempt. The scorn of an angry saint almost. Now and then when I have received that look of hers I have wondered if I could still keep going. I took a rapid step back and bowed my head a little, as if to show that any insolence she detected in me was just a case of mistaken identity. We had to find a way to carry on, that was all I wanted to convey.

The priest's arms were beginning to flail about. The handsome goodwill he was obviously so proud of – we all were – was growing threadbare. I caught his eye and mouthed the words 'so sorry', but if he saw me he did not respond. The whole occasion was about to fall to bits. What did he expect?

'OK, well, that's great, I mean you've known her for fifteen years, more than half your lifetime, so let's go with Sheila then. I know, why don't you ask and I'll nip out and get her a coffee, if you like, to ... to help her, you know, everyone likes a coffee, don't they, before a big ...? Shall I get you one too? I'll do that.'

'OK,' Eleanor said in her ice voice.

I deposited Lily into Father Pat's startled arms and walked to the café next to the Sainsbury's, where there was a queue in front of the long glass cabinet behind which two waitresses were buttering fawn-coloured bread. A small basket of dimpled plastic oranges was balanced on the counter, a charity tin – Save the Children. What about the mothers? One of the waitresses tilted her head at me, and although it wasn't my turn I asked if they did coffees to take away and she said no. I told her it was a bit of an emergency and I wouldn't normally ask but we needed to revive someone fast who was under the weather, in order to be godmother at a christening over the road that was already promising to be, threatening to be, fraying at its edges, quite likely to disintegrate altogether, or implode – did I really say all that? – and the extremely nice priest was running out of patience with everyone, not his fault, but ... and a tear jumped out of my eye because there was only so much you could take sometimes, and as luck would have it something in my voice made a deep appeal with the woman behind the counter and I was no longer a demanding customer, I was a situation, and that meant different rules came into play. I could have sunk down on my knees to thank her. She made me milky coffees for Eleanor and Sheila in pristine polystyrene cups and I brought them back to the church, hot mauve liquid bubbling through the tiny holes in the lids, scalding drips on the inside of my thumbs. Good for them to get a few calories down them as well, little stick insects, stick people, sick people.

Sheila's boyfriend saw me come back into the church and began to rouse her gently and I handed him the coffee and he removed the lid, held the cup up to her mouth, blew on it for her and fed it to her in thin little sips, his other arm coiled round her back. He was careful with her, fielding her slumps and stumbling. I was glad she was with someone nurturing, even if he was more than twice her age.

'So.' I gave her my best invigorating smile – my voice had file paper in it, ring binders, hole punches, sticks of chalk. 'Shall I explain how it's all going to go? When he calls us up, the priest, you and me,' I pointed at her and then at myself, 'we'll just go over to the font together, over there,' I gestured again, 'and we'll say the things the priest tells us. We just repeat the words after him. That sound all right?'

'Yes, miss,' she said.

'Call me Ruth. Go on. Please. We're not at school any more.' She looked doubtful.

I half wondered if we could ask Father Pat to be godfather.

We got through it somehow. The best moment was when me, Ben, Sheila and Eleanor all rejected the glamour of evil. Lily looked at me aghast. Not on my account, she seemed to say. I caught Father Pat's eye and he caught mine and his pupils were pitched between humour and despair. 'You know we'd better laugh or we might cry because *I* don't know what to do,' his eyes whispered – or even what the *hell* to do or possibly what the *fuck* – and it was so intimate suddenly it was almost for a moment as though none of us was wearing any clothes – maybe I have underestimated religion – in any case I had to look away. Did Lily actually roll her eyes then? Could a baby do that? She was so comical. It was a brilliant idea to be a baby and laugh a great deal more than you cried.

It was time for me to do the reading. I unhooked Sheila's arm from mine, helped her back into her seat so she could rest. I always got the girls at school to learn a poem on Friday afternoons. It will be a lovely wallpaper for your life, I told them, especially at in-between moments when you can't get off to sleep, when you're waiting for the bus or nervous about an important meeting at work, when you're feeding your babies you can just run through beautiful things in your mind to lift yourself, when you're about to take your curtain call at Stratford-upon-Avon. Often I would learn one with them too. I had 'Piping down the Valleys Wild', Blake's poem of innocence, up my sleeve. That was childish, joyous, baptismal. Good. I stood, confidently, about to begin, and then suddenly I was unsure that its glee and cheer were really what was called for, even though it contained a few tears. I needed something more stringent, a manifesto.

I remembered a song from my mother's funeral. It was one of the final things. I almost didn't make it to the end. Eleanor was a couple of months old then and she and I were living in two rooms that smelled strongly of laundry that the woman downstairs boiled in a huge saucepan on her stove, bleach and scorch round the clock, so that the walls and the staircase were permanently sweating. I was a liquid mass of grief myself: milk, tears, exhaustion. I used to sit feeding Eleanor remembering my mother's sleeping sounds, her steady breathing and her lovely face – femininity that was its own reward – birdsong welling up from the street and bright chips of children's playing noises.

I was thirty but I didn't know anything. Eleanor's father put in an appearance perhaps an hour a week, keeping his coat on, eyes trained on the door. Sometimes he wouldn't sit down.

It was a hymn I chose then, a hymn about kindness. My mother hadn't had an easy life and I wanted to acknowledge it; correct it, offer compensation. I stood at the lectern again now, for Lily, glad of its support and the way it shielded me and I began to sing. The sound was thin at first, like a shy choirboy, but then I came into my own a little bit. The priest stood to my right, mouthing the words alongside me like a holy stage mother. Lily wriggled in her mother's arms. I felt *my* mother with me too, at my side, on my side. It was to the tune of 'The Londonderry Air' or 'Danny Boy'. I didn't know who the 'I' character in the song was, whether it was me, or my mother, or God or Eleanor or Lily or . . . or . . . Was I singing an apology to the human race? Some days the way you parodied yourself could be quite breathtaking. I smiled.

I would be true, for there are those who trust me;
I would be pure, for there are those who care;
I would be strong, for there is much to suffer;
I would be brave, for there is much to dare.

I would be friend of all – the foe, the friendless;
I would be giving, and forget the gift;
I would be humble, for I know my weakness;
I would look up, and laugh, and love, and live.

I took my seat again. 'Miss,' Sheila was saying, 'miss,' and she squeezed my arm. I hoped Ben and Eleanor didn't mind I had introduced notes of sadness. They had introduced them to me.

'Very nice,' the priest said. Jean Reynolds from school would have been impressed. She would have nudged me sharply in the ribs and stage-whispered, 'Good job!' Even Eleanor smiled. Why was Ben's mother not here? Wasn't this whole thing her idea? Had there been some last-minute clash or boycott? Eleanor once said Ben's mum didn't think Lily was his. Something about her colouring being off, apparently.

Afterwards Lily giggled and made free with her cuddles. It was so generous of her to think everything was funny. It might just be me, but I sometimes found babies a bit cynical round the edges. Their been-here-before auras often registered as smug. No other species considered itself so distinguished while being so glaringly generic, surely? But Lily was civilised and high-spirited. She met the world with wonder and awe. She was aware of her strengths but she didn't think she knew everything like some babies. She understood that in the grand scheme of things she had been born yesterday. I was in love with her, I suppose. I was making myself smile again. Lily's outlook was healthy, she was very taken with life, squeezing delight out of a mushroom or a cotton reel, pretty amazing when you consider she was half poisoned before she was even born.

I felt arrows of rage rising in me, fraught images spreading like bloodstains. There's no point, I told myself. I reached for the ordinary decoys. It won't get you anywhere. Think of the outcome you want and make sure you are moving towards it. Got to be practical. That was what I always told the girls at school. There is so much in life that doesn't matter, so many things that hold you back, hem you in and throw you off the scent of what's important. Don't get too bogged down in things that don't count or things you cannot influence, and specifically don't worry too much about making sure others know you're in the right, because it so easily gets in the way of what you want and need. Become an expert at shrugging most of life off and free yourself for what really interests you. Hone your focus. Don't bother with cleaning or tidiness beyond basic hygiene. Don't make your appearance your primary concern. It will zap all your creativity. Be as self-sufficient as you dare. Sometimes you hold more strength when people don't know what you think or feel, so be very careful whom you confide in. People can run with your difficulties when you least expect it, distort them, relish them even, and before you know it they're not yours any more. Respect your privacy. And earn your own money or you'll lack power. Take good care of your friendships, nurture them and they'll strengthen you. Don't turn frowning at the defects of other people into a hobby, delicious though it may be; it poisons you. Read every day – it is a practice that dignifies humans. Become a great reader of books and it will help you with reality, you'll more easily grasp the truth of things and that will set you up for life. And don't expose your brain to low-quality art forms because there will be a certain measure of pollution.

We all had our sermons to give.

The light was lacy in the church. Ben and Eleanor seemed to have lost interest in the proceedings and kept wandering off into the street. I minded the way they were so unapologetic, although it had a certain high style, you could say. There was a dark passage at the back of the building, partially covered by corrugated iron – they were probably making themselves at home there. We had reached a standstill. Father Pat had lost his nerve, that was clear. 'Where are they?' he mouthed to me, bright smile collapsing; he had been left holding the baby for the second time. He was standing by the altar and although the light around him was delicate, his face ennobled by narrow slits of dappled sun, he could not quite shake off the fact that he looked like a camp oil painting entitled *The Reluctant Father*.

'Yes, they do seem vague,' I said, lifting Lily from his arms, with some tutting and clucking in my general atmosphere. 'They're so unpredictable, the young people.' I didn't know what to say to him.

When I was a child, I was mad for God. I prayed to the Virgin every evening to improve my character. I prayed to the Holy Spirit to make my mother happy. I went on a retreat one year with some other children to a centre near Borehamwood. There were red-brick huts and hundreds of conifer trees. We stayed up late sucking cherry-flavoured sweets at the back of the coach in our pyjamas, chatting with the driver, who handed round a bottle of gin. My friends Suzy and Marion said that Jesus loved us so much and even before we were born he thought of us all the time with immense tenderness and we were silent at the vastness of it. The driver was visibly moved. 'Give us a cuddle, girls?' he said, and Marion had compassion and gave him some kisses on the lips, and afterwards, giddy from the gin, we wobbled our way down the bus's steep steps, tiptoeing across the gravel courtyard in our slippers, feeling our way back to the dormitory in the dark. We sat on our beds wrapped up in paisley eiderdowns, measuring all the steps involved in perfecting ourselves.

Day's done. Gone the sun.

Christine in gleaming conker-coloured moccasins – couldn't have been more than thirteen at the time – said, 'Of course, God will always be more important to those with absent fathers.'

29

We had the last part of the service without the parents in attendance. Lily didn't seem to mind. Sheila's boyfriend came to the font to support her and the sunlight flashed appreciatively against his gold cufflinks. It was going through the motions really at that point; me and Sheila linked arms again carefully. Her bones felt light and brittle, twice as old as mine. Afterwards Ben and Eleanor wandered back in. Someone had a camera and took a roll of film and I asked if I could get it developed myself, promised I'd send off for lots of sets of prints, but they said it was all right. There didn't seem to be a plan for a meal or anything, a cup of tea, a cake, bunches of flowers. Ben settled Lily in the pram at this point and I thought her on the verge of sleep after her triumph.

I couldn't put it off any longer. Eleanor came towards me, but there were filaments of shame in her eyes that alarmed me. She was sensitive and when she saw her expression strike me as a sort of injury she said, 'Oh no, Mum, please,' and I said, 'It's OK, love,' and she said, 'I am sorry, Mum, it was kind of all over the place, wasn't it?' and I said, 'Not at all. Was lovely. Well done. Come here,' and she gave me a big hug and let me reassure her. I don't know if I'm good and I don't know if I'm evil but I knew what I wanted so I loosened myself from her and went and fetched Lily. She was sleeping flat out in her pram now, a subtle sort of smile on her, so I wheeled her over and I beckoned to Ben to come over too, and I said, 'Ben, Eleanor, I know it's been slightly chaotic, but what a lovely occasion. Don't you think? Can't have been easy to organise, I know. Congratulations to you both, to all three of you really.' Ben looked at me and opened his mouth as if to challenge, but I held my own. 'Now, what I was thinking. Would you like me to take Lily home for the night, for the weekend even, a few days or so, and you could have a break, a bit of time to yourselves, catch up on your sleep. A week?'

'No, Mum,' Eleanor said, but Ben was looking more alert suddenly.

'Oh, and I've got her present as well to give you. I didn't know what to get. What do you give the person who has nothing! So I thought you could choose something she'd really like, for when she's older, or if you need anything now, or save it up for later on,' I said, and I handed them the envelope of Sickert money, four thousand pounds, warm and me-smelling, and kissed them both as if to bless the gift. They smiled, although Eleanor was beginning to look a little bored, but when they opened the envelope and saw what was inside, in under a second there was almost steam coursing out of their mouths and their nostrils, and their eyes bulged, not quite like common frogs, or I don't know, cartoon conmen, but almost. They both nodded again and Ben said carefully, 'You are right, it has been exhausting this whole thing. You are so kind and thoughtful.'

'We'll buy her something lovely, Mum,' Eleanor said, 'and open a bank account for her and everything.'

'So can I have her then? Few days? A week . . . ?'

Ben was nodding. Eleanor shrugged, which was often how she agreed with me anyway.

I took a deep breath, but it wasn't over yet, because when I looked up, I saw that Father Pat had witnessed the whole thing. He looked at me a bit savagely, his eyebrows raised, his forehead knitted with a measure of disdain, and it was possible he may have shaken his head at me severely, without any fellow feeling, or even irony, and there was a flash of stern intent in his lips, which seemed to have thinned, and he raised his hand as though to ask a question or object or even smite me for what I had done, but I stared him down and his disgust – I wasn't a bad person and he was brand new to all this and was in no position to judge anyone. He didn't know them as I did; he had not witnessed their mad omissions and neglect, the way their contempt could bear down on you with full force when the truth was it was they who were red-handed. He hadn't done those long flickering nights in the hospital with Lily for the first weeks of her life when she cried for something no one would give her.

All perspective, the passing of time and the scale of things, had broken down then. That huge half-Victorian building was swallowing me whole into its strange city with its own gravity, its own overheated laws and cruel light. The sky-blue and royal-blue and navy and lilac nurses, brisk footsteps against the bright lino, weary, brave, chattering, sugar, cigarettes. I existed on plastic coffee from the machine and stale newspapers, leaping out of my seat whenever anyone walked by, sleeping rarely, scarcely changing my damp clothes or going for a pee I was so terrified of something bad happening if I took my eye off things. I could feel the undercurrent of my nerves pulsating; love and anxiety plaited with fright. The stiffness of the air, light, dimmed light, half-darkness, space, light again. Eleanor and Ben came. Not as often as they should. Terrible of me to think that. Obviously it was worse for them, but was it, though? Lily lay in her see-through box behind a glass wall. 'Somebody needs to be cuddling her,' I told anyone who would listen, shaking my head, shaking my heart. I asked the nurse to give her a pale-blue knitted square I had made her and then get Eleanor to hold it next to her skin, so that they would learn each other's smell, swap it back and forth every few hours, but the nurse said they had to be more careful with hygiene at this stage. Eleanor's eyelids were white and hard and swollen. With me she was tough and remote. I tried to be kindly to her shame, but who would do the same for me? Ben seemed to shrink whenever he saw me, retreating deep into himself, his face blazing pale, his skin flaking all over his clothes.

Outside, the sun died every night and I sometimes stood for a second and watched it slink from the picture windows on the landing by the lifts, counting the lights threading across London. The sky whitened at the start of each day but I wasn't sure you could rely on it. All our luck was in Lily's hands. After a time the doctors informed me there was to be a change of plan. Lily would have tiny amounts of morphine because she was having trouble sleeping and feeding and she was weak and in distress. I watched the morphine going into her system; the near-instant relief it brought. That was dark theatre; my hand splayed across my mouth. I grabbed a nurse: 'What if that's all she wants now?' I tried to keep my voice down. If they thought you were any kind of troublemaker, they could send you away.

I rubbed hibiscus soap into my hands, counting to a hundred. I did it again. An unliveable moment stretched out before me. I forbade myself from speaking after that. I knew the facts were incoherent, as the detailed accounts of battles always were. I couldn't be trusted. Some of the babies through the glass were peaceful in the fluorescent air. Some only a little bigger than my hand, raw-looking, chicken-legged, bandaged and wired, so delicate. Strange curled sea creatures, huge black grape eyes. One smiled in its sleep, but it wasn't my one. My one was crying without movement or sound. I wished I could climb in there beside her. The doctors were severe and wise with me. The nurse reappeared at my side with a small pleated paper cup of white pills. 'You'll be all right,' she said, which was kind. She held my hand for a few seconds. Let it go. On to the next.

I turned and walked briskly to the foot of the church, tucked the christening blanket around Lily's body as she didn't seem to come with a coat or anything, and steered the grubby handle of the pram onto the street. At the weekend I could take her to the zoo, I thought. To Brighton to watch the wind whip the waves. Maybe there would be a white Christmas – a hushed early morning with that strange feathery light. I saw Lily waving her arms in delight as thick snowflakes landed on her nose and chin, her lips pursed intently, her fingers clawing the frozen jigsaw pieces. I was mapping things carefully. Eleanor was reading before she went to school and she could write and sew and knit and crochet and draw from life, after a fashion, and make basic paper dolls and paper clothes to dress them. I still had some of her beautiful pictures somewhere, in a yellow folder, dense with details.

I made my way up the high street, manoeuvring the pram in and out of bustling lunch-hour pedestrians. Lily woke for a moment and her steady blue ironical eyes seemed to take in her surroundings and then they took the measure of me. There was so much gaiety in her expression and I tried to harvest a bit of it.

Courage could be hard sometimes, manual labour almost, but not this. I suddenly felt like one of those daredevil stunt motorcyclists, soaring over sixteen double-decker buses, through ragged hoops of fire.

Wheeeeeee!

THREE

For a plump roasting chicken knead the butter with the tarragon leaves, half a clove of chopped garlic, salt and pepper. Put this inside the bird, which should be well coated with olive oil.

I have long admired Elizabeth David's prose style and thought of her up there with the other Elizabeths, Taylor and Bowen (if that wasn't sacrilege). Her madeleines recipe included the following stark warning: *Faith is essential; should the moulds be overfilled, the mixture will spread sideways, the result will be a failure.*

I brought some in for the sixth form on my birthday.

'I'm not being funny, but they don't taste of much, do they, miss.'

Jean Reynolds at school has started giving the sixth form updates from her marriage counselling sessions and my old chat about the Elizabeths could hardly compete. The girls adored it when she regaled them with episodes from her life. It was quite a clever way of showing them respect, trusting them with things their own mothers wouldn't dream of divulging. It made them feel mature and valued, hard feelings to come by during adolescence certainly. Treating them as equals. I enjoyed seeing Jean through her pupils' eyes. She was daring. She said things like 'Alan's started one of his affairs again. Of course the whistling's the giveaway' and 'I don't know about you girls, but I *love* to go to bed with Othello.' If I was in her form and it was me on the receiving end of such mad bulletins, I'd have been tempted to say, 'You do know, miss, that he killed his wife?'

'So, so literal, Ruth,' she would scold with one of her grand, dismissive arm gestures. You really needed more stature for a move like that.

The girls loved lessons with hints of transgression or high drama, but I preferred them to think that I was dull. Mine was an earnest, conventional home life, quiet, boring, and it was in what we were reading that all the secrets and colour lay. If they witnessed wilder scenes from my domestic set-up, they would have watched transfixed – their own bouts and clashes with their mums blown up a thousandfold, *miles* better than the telly – but what we read would have been completely lost. I had always been calm outwardly.

I severed the chicken skin while I was pushing the tarragon butter up against the breast, which made me angry. I was cooking nervously – the pressure of moral forces, was it? Something like that. Bad timing in any case. I tucked the pale potatoes round the bird, burned my hand slightly as I slid the tin into the oven, held my crimson fingers under the tap. Some days all of life was kill or cure.

'We're doing well, Mum,' Eleanor said when she rang me a few days after the funeral to ask for Lily. Not the funeral – God almighty! – the christening.

'Oh, I'm so pleased to hear that, that's brilliant, well done.' There was only solid cheer in my voice. I needed to play things carefully. I had a sense of strong alarm. The chicken bolstered me slightly. Safety in numbers, was it? As if that made sense.

Lily woke after a long nap with clownish pink discs on her cheeks; must be teething. I still had a bottle of oil of cloves from twenty-five years ago. She had one tooth already – a china ornament in a small red display cabinet – I boasted to Jean. I put her on her tartan blanket, propped her with cushions, arranged some plastic saucepans and spoons and cups next to her that we kept in the red colander – her 'cookings'. Eleanor used to march my cotton reels up and down in little regiments for hours on end on that same scratched patch of kitchen floor. Lily would be crawling soon. Oh-oh. I smiled at her and she gave me such a sympathetic look in return.

At five thirty, I strapped the carrycot into the back of the car with Lily nestled in it and wedged the hot chicken in the boot still in its tin. I had a scarf for Eleanor I had knitted in the summer, cream, orange and fawn zigzag stripes. I had *My First Book of Nature*, which Fran had sent me for Lily from work. I fetched the orange bucket I kept the cleaning things in from under the sink, propping it against the passenger seat, wrapping the book in a clean J-cloth.

In the car, Lily did that funny ba-ba singing that she does and I joined in. She had an oddly earnest look when she sang and sometimes closed her eyes in the way serious-hearted classical musicians do. It was very comical but I knew not to laugh because she was sincere. It started to rain heavily, hitting the windows in great dirty strokes. Eleanor's roof wasn't brilliant. I'd had it repaired before Lily was born but the roofer refused to come back when it started to leak two weeks later. He knew he didn't have to. You couldn't really make anyone do anything when you lived as she lived. You lost a lot of ordinary entitlements.

I drove to Eleanor's street, where lights and scenes of Sunday life flashed inside the rows of houses, squares of yellow warm against the beginnings of the dark. It was a better street than mine, half-stuccoed houses, teatime violins, the skies solid with horse chestnut trees, their large open-handed leaves squished and mashed into the paving stones. It was a street without visible drama, without the slamming of car doors all through the evening, the angry bouts and shouts I was used to.

She had spoken of improvements with some ceremony on the telephone. I never knew what I was allowed to think. I parked abruptly, peered into the mirror, gave my hair a few rough swipes with a comb, patted down my fringe. There were practical things to negotiate. I wasn't going to be able to carry Lily and the tin with the chicken at the same time, or was I? The main thing was . . . I stared hard at what seemed a cartoon equation. The main thing, the only thing, was to leave the chicken and to keep the babe.

I managed to loop Lily under my right arm and hold the tin with the chicken and the potatoes on the flat of my left hand, my thumb hooked firmly over the lip of the dish. They were both warm, both weighing about the same. I was well balanced, if that wasn't too great a claim. I was instant family life, dinner and a baby, a comprehensive delivery service. Somebody's dream. Lily wriggled but at least the chicken kept still as I walked up the path through the front garden that the long-suffering downstairs neighbour kept neatly. There were the last of the hydrangeas, crisped heads heavy with rainfall, necks bent almost to the ground.

I put the chicken down on the doorstep, trying to keep the rain off its back with the edge of my coat, and rang the bell marked *Top Flat*, picked the tin up again and waited. I could smell the meaty vapours on Lily's head, sweet milky gravy. I rang again and then I knocked. I've had all the feelings, the bitter flashes of contempt, the thick animal pity. The world was Eleanor's widow, I sometimes thought.

A few more minutes passed and I called up to the window. I could see dim shapes moving about up there, figures leaning against the wall. Lily was getting bored. 'Here's the front door. Rat-a-tat-tat. Here's the doorbell. Ding-dong, who's there? I remember teaching your mum her animal noises like it was yesterday. What noise does a cow make? Mooo. What noise does a horse make? Clop clop clop clop. What noise does a cup of tea make, and then she'd do a brisk sip followed by a long sighing ahh sound, very comical. You'd really laugh. And you know she was walking at nine months. That's unusual. Quite distinguished, in the baby ... *department*? The baby *kingdom*?'

Lily smiled indulgently. *The baby kingdom* – were we elevating it to a religion now?

Eleanor, finally, was at the door. 'Hello there!' I said, lighting myself up. She didn't look bad. I had a rush of gratitude. She was in one of her old voluminous dark jerseys, chewed-looking cuffs, crumpled white shirt tails peeping out below, made me think of ship's sails for some reason. Medieval-looking jeans hanging off her. She had washed her hair, which shimmered with wet. She didn't seem affronted at all. I was pleased. 'Hi Mum,' she said, but she spoke without any warmth at all, as though she was saying 'curtain' or 'gas bill'. I tried to get a sense from her eyes, from her mouth, from her face what kind of evening we were in for, but it was too dingy to tell. And she did not enjoy being scrutinised for signs of life. Who could blame her? I wished I could be more immune to the effect my behaviour had on her: how her reactions struck my features and how her face then responded to the rapid contortions she saw in mine. We were a mirrored room with hundreds of reflections flashing back and back and back. I knew my constant search for glints of hope was tasteless, but I couldn't stop myself.

Besides, both of us, because of this mad dance we did, tended to have feelings that were unreliable. Fractured thoughts rounded up to the next number, forced understandings, false intuition. We needed them, I think, and they were linked to an instinct for peace. We sometimes reassured each other to gain a bit of soft-ness and safety and confidence, a sense of ease that wasn't quite truthful; a neighbourliness of spirit now and then could work for a while, get you over the smaller stumbling blocks. I knew I could be guilty of not letting myself see things.

We were walking up the stairs, Eleanor in front. She was frag-ile and bird-limbed from behind, sidestepping awkwardly. I'd give anything to have you less spindly and evasive – I killed the thought. I hated the way my feelings had to go out of their way to avoid attention when I was with her.

'What's that?' she said, peering back uncertainly in the direction of the chicken.

'It's a chicken!'

'What's it for?'

'What's it for? For tonight. For eating. For food.'

'OK,' she said, as though I had invented a whole new pastime. I smiled frankly.

'What's the green stuff?'

'Tarragon, Elizabeth David. Sainsbury's does it, not all the time, though – s'nice. Quite nice, grassy, bit like aniseed. Are you hungry?'

'Later. Maybe.'

'Are you tired?'

'Yeah. Had some people round.'

'That sounds fun.' *Fun?*

In the downstairs hallway things had looked quite ordered, small piles of post and a dark green carpet, forest green, velvety. The higher you climbed, though, the worse it got, the last flight of stairs riddled with stains and so on, clumps of black bin bags to either side of the runner, a stage set of dereliction, white textured wallpaper crusty with damp, fag ends and burns, cardboard boxes, stale air, alarm. God, they were brazen. When we reached her landing, the banister was barely clinging on. A bitter smell, old milk possibly, and underneath something musty, sweet rotten wood. It might just have been the smell of festering rubbish in my head, of course. I sighed deeply and took my bottom lip in my teeth. She *despised* me when I did things like that. Her mouth hardened, brutish and wintry. She hadn't even acknowledged the baby. That made me sad.

'Here we are,' she said, no shame, no pride in her voice, no despair, no anything. Possibly a grain or two of resignation, possibly not even that as she pushed the door. She didn't want her reactions monitored and tracked.

Lily wore a doubtful expression, searching and curious. She clung to me and it made her heavier suddenly. I felt that she was trying to guard her privacy. My forearm ached under the weight of the chicken also, but there wasn't anywhere sensible to set it down.

On the floorboards between the sofa and an armchair there were some plates of old food with rusty tea bags, fag ends floating in a blue and white mug, a lighter, Coke and beer cans, cigarette papers, an abandoned card game, metal takeaway containers with brownish noodles, clotted and glistening, a TV guide, a book of matches, some flowers in a jug, their stalks swollen and slimy, beginning to stink. A burnt spoon. A man asked me if I wanted to sit down. The room was so gloomy with its one faint corner bulb I hadn't seen him. 'Oh thanks,' I said, 'that's kind,' but I didn't take up his offer. I was imagining Eleanor screaming at me for composing the phrase 'your squalid little still life' in my head. I was used to tiptoeing round things. I knew my thoughts could flare up against me, wounded and beseeching. If I was pleased with her or if I despaired, she found me equally hard to stomach. I really didn't know what was fair, let alone what was allowed.

I went into the little square kitchen – that wasn't too bad. There was a new unopened packet of forty-eight nappies on top of the fridge, which impressed me. I put the chicken down on the cooker, moved Lily from my right hip to my left; it was lucky, in a way, she wasn't heavier. I put some plates and mugs in the sink, emptied the ashtrays into the bin without looking at its contents, picked two withered apples and a mouldy lemon out of a glass bowl. I rinsed my hand on the slip of black-veined soap, wiped it on my skirt, got some tissues out of my pocket, wetted them, squirted on some Fairy Liquid and swabbed the worktop. I washed some plates, pretty hard with just one hand, draping a scrap of towel over my shoulder to wipe them down against myself. I set the worst saucepans to soak – the frying pan looked as though it was from the Bronze Age. My own state of mind was unclear. I would have to put Lily down in order to do the floor, fetch the bucket and rags from the car, but there was nowhere for her. I could come back another time maybe. I opened the cupboard above the sink to put the cups away and saw ten small jars of baby food stacked in a pyramid: beef and carrot casserole, lamb and tender vegetables, sweetcorn with chicken, apple and pear pudding. That changed things. I leant against the wall for a minute, holding Lily tightly to me, soothing myself with a stagey sing-song voice and several 'all right thens' and 'I know, I knows'. Amazing the way you could be patronising to yourself and resent it even as you required it.

I kissed her a few times on the head. Not too much. I couldn't stand what was going to happen.

There was a strong, cool breeze in the little kitchen around waist height. 'Getting cold,' I said too loudly, to no one, and as if to prove it I knocked on the half-closed door of the bedroom opposite, gently pushed it open, wandered in, head down, went over to the window, pulled it shut. I was carrying out an unplanned inspection, I realised; I was often slow on the uptake where Eleanor was concerned, the last to know my own thoughts and actions even. There was a deep pile of old coats lying on a ticking mattress under the window. I hoped it was a pile of coats. It was all very still. Lily shivered in my arms and started to whimper. I thought I ought to investigate lightly, peel back the layers of clothing to see what was underneath, but I knew it wasn't good. The atmosphere was heavy, very hard to carry suddenly. It was the coldest part of the room. The smell wasn't right. I stopped breathing. I closed my eyes for a few seconds. There was a shoe peeping out. God almighty. It wasn't decent in life to receive other people's difficulties like an insult or a weapon, I knew better than that, but I thought I was going to be sick. I swallowed it down.

Eleanor's head peeped round the door. 'You wanna tea?' she said. I could see her mood was brighter now; she was a bit blithe suddenly, festive at her edges. The last of the light had gone and she was always better after dark. Everything about the day was too harsh for her, the sharp squalor of morning, the shabby haze of afternoon. She suffered from nervousness also. It was natural. It was as hard for her as it was for me.

'Another time,' I said brightly, trying to sound encouraging. 'Um, I think I . . . '

'You OK?'

'Yeah. Just, it's just, I probably ought to be off soon. Sorry I can't stay and help you out tonight. Is Ben about?'

She smiled. 'Be back in a minute. Gone up the shops.'

'OK. I just wanted to ask him some—'

'You got loads of marking to do?'

That was a great gift. Yeah. 'A ton of it. You wouldn't believe.'

'You are good,' she said, which made me laugh.

'Thank you!'

I kissed her at the bedroom doorway, put my free arm out and fed it cautiously round her back, holding my breath like a teenage boy with a girl. She twitched and shivered slightly but she didn't object. I gave her shoulder a series of friendly pats, which she accepted manfully. She admired the Fair Isle Lily was wearing, a present from Sarah from a job lot of old clothes. Then she put out her arms to take her from me, but at that moment Ben came back from wherever it was, and we were very crowded on the little patch of brown carpet tile suddenly with two doors open and four people including Lily in a tiny space and eight elbows and their bony ankles not to mention all the personalities, and I ducked out of Eleanor's way onto the landing outside their front door. Ben was dangling a blue-and-white-striped carrier bag from his wrist. A bottle of wine, two cartons of baby milk, a peppermint Aero. He looked eager and greeted me warmly and I followed him back into the flat, into the tiny kitchen, the sliding door rattling shut behind me, Lily clamped to my chest.

'Ben, can you listen to me for a moment so I can tell you something. Is that . . . ? Sorry to—'

'Yeah.'

'I think there's someone in your bedroom who's not doing so well. It could be quite bad, I don't know. He's not moving at all. Could you see if it's all right? I've no idea. Might be nothing. Just . . . it doesn't look good. I—'

'Shit,' he said. 'Shit. Shit, shit.' He was blinking rapidly, coming to. 'That's all right,' he said. 'It's ALL right. NO problem. I can—'

'You want me to help you?'

He shook his head. 'No, you're all right.'

I called out a small 'Bye then' and started to make my way down the stairs.

'Hey! You're not taking Lily?' He came out onto the landing and called after me suddenly, and Lily and I both raised our chins to meet his eyes in the stairwell but we didn't stop walking.

'You know what,' I called back up to him calmly, 'I think I might.'

We ran down the rest of the green stairs and I drove to the end of the street and parked abruptly. We sat in the car for a while to recover ourselves, doors locked, and my breaths came very fast and my hands were trembling. I reached into the back for Lily and brought her onto my knee. I was shaking hard then and she started to mewl and I sang her to sleep against my chest and I think I sang myself also. The next thing I knew an ambulance siren was wailing right next to us, the traffic parting effortfully to let it through.

'Home, James,' I murmured to Lily, popping her back into the carrycot.

A couple of weeks earlier, Jean Reynolds had frowned with what I took for fellow feeling in the staff room and said, 'You know, I could not lead your life.' She saw the hurt strike my face right away, drips of rejection smearing my cheeks, and she apologised formally. She dropped a postcard into my pigeonhole the following day; a painting of Pushkin wounded on his deathbed. *Me with my big foot in my evil mouth AGAIN* she'd written in green ink. *Forgive me?* But sitting in the car fleeing clumsily a scene I didn't fully understand, her words were comforting. Jean often minimised things. Pain and difficulties, for example, she faced staunchly. You had to *fight with all your might*, she believed, arranging yourself as a pilgrim soldier in relation to life, against the world, defiant and livid, even at eleven twenty on a dreary Thursday morning, but I was glad she did not require the same of me. That she saw my situation was impossible. These things you appreciated all the more when you had been completely invalidated as a mother.

My focus was narrowing. I had planned for this moment. You cannot leave the child with them. You cannot leave the child with them. I was used to having Lily at short notice, tearing into work with caked milk on my shirt, clumps of egg, damp trails of sieved pear, baby porridge, baby snot, baby love. She had El's old high-chair at mine with its own white tray table, she had an assortment of toys, she had, well – me.

It was true I had helped them to look better and stronger. False impressions, necessary in their way. After Lily came home from the hospital I was at their flat every day, before and after work, cooking, cleaning in my lunch hour sometimes – the skin rough and scaly, half scoured from my hands. Nerves red-raw also, and you couldn't get cream for that. I brought fruit and crusty loaves and ironed baby clothes and muslin squares piled up in the drawers for the health visitors. There were handymen in to fix things. I got a cheap set of *Encyclopaedia Britannica* with volume N–Q missing but that only lasted a week. Granny sat knitting an oasis of competence and calm when the social workers descended. Click clack, click clack, like a steady old grandmother clock. A safe pair of hands. Hello! A fawn Napoleonic-looking bonnet with a dignified tassel. Hello! Another for the summer in lightweight wool, pale blue. The older social worker was enchanted: 'It's like something out of Jane Austen!' A state-of-the-art electric steam steriliser – Argos's best – they'd not seen its like before. Practically cooked the dinner, we laughed.

And always I kept a lightness to my tone, a tentative, cautiously optimistic atmosphere: 'We're doing well, I think, yes, I am a bit heartened.' 'They are getting the hang of it, but how do *you* think we're doing?' 'Perfect timing – we're just about to take out the sponge cake. Do you prefer raspberry or apricot jam?' I put up two shelves and arranged puzzles and soft toys on those shelves, I made curtains, ordered a blackout blind. Bought the pram and the cot and the bedding. 'It seems to me the baby is helping them turn themselves round. I want to do everything to try and make this work.' Odd those times in life when telling the truth sounded like deceit. I routinely cleaned out the bathroom cabinet because the health visitors always poked about in there. Lily was up to date on all her jabs and check-ups. The team came every other day at the start so this process was repeated on a cycle. There was a box inside a box inside another box under the bed. For unmentionables. Out of sight, out of mind. I often brought Lily over to mine at weekends. Odd to be so proud and so furious with yourself all at once. At certain times I felt almost too embarrassed to exist.

Lily was not going to have a *poultice* childhood, a mending service, scrappy and provisional. I wouldn't *step in*. She was going to get the most anyone could give. They had had their chance. I was ambitious for her. She was herself, you could see it on her face where there was plainly visible a tenacity of purpose to her. I was going to have everything solid and substantial, get a proper residence order. Parental responsibility documentation. There was to be no question of drawn-out negotiations. Pass the parcel. Middle of the night. I wasn't doing that again. There would be no more money either. I had long lists written in a little notebook if they were needed. Bad things that made me ashamed of myself.

It was Jean who told me to document everything. 'A book of evidence?' I objected flatly. 'No, no, no. She doesn't deserve that.'

'I don't think you understand. She is ill and this is an illness that comes with an inevitable ethical decline. It's a symptom. Once you've got the baby, they will have you over a barrel.'

'What are you talking about? Who is this *they*?'

'They get you to fall in love with her then they come in the night, they threaten to take the baby off you unless you give them all your money.'

'You've been watching too much TV, Jean. And I am already in love with her. And also – what money?!'

'Well. Maybe … But just write down everything. It will strengthen you.'

'Must I?'

'Uh-huh.'

I could be hard-hearted. I've rarely shown it in life, but it was in me.

Without the baby they might go downhill very fast.

Lily could think of her parents as a madcap weekend aunt and uncle, eccentric as circus folk, or astronauts, their hearts in the right place but their heads in the clouds. Elsewhere and distracted but funny and loving, clever certainly, a little unrealistic about life, careless possibly, children themselves, which was why we were making the decisions this end. Harsher lines could be drawn but I was keen to avoid them. When she was older, I would explain that with the best will in the world they had been too unwell to look after her. There was sadness but it needn't be presented as a crime scene. They were coping poorly, not poorly from the viewpoint of another's judgement, as in badly, but poorly meaning 'with great difficulty'.

'What you going to do with her when you're at work?' Jean said. 'If you do manage to get her?'

For once, I had an answer. 'I've got this neighbour, Kay, who's a childminder. Retired now, but she used to be a nurse at Northwick Park. Her husband's a butler at a big hotel in the West End. Grosvenor House, is that the one on Park Lane? Seen her out and about with the double buggy loads of times. She's got a lovely atmosphere. She sings "Molly Malone" to the toddlers as she pushes them down the street. Points out the names of the trees. "That's a sycamore, not the most exciting tree in the world, but as I always say, it's a tree you can rely on."'

'Oh.'

'Just be two and a half days a week, same as I'm doing now, and only in term time, thirty-seven weeks a year. And she'll be asleep for a quarter of that time. So ... And it's just till she's ready for nursery. I called round there. It's all pretty cosy. She's up for it.'

'And what's that going to cost?'

'It's doable, just, if I'm careful.'

Jean nodded. She knew I was sparing by nature. 'How anyone can sleep in woolly tights!' she shook her head at me once.

'Don't knock it till you've tried it, Jean.'

It was enough of a plan for week one. We drew up outside my

49

flat, and in the street there was some altercation between a half-dressed girl and a fat bald man in a car. The streets here were getting worse by the minute; they were ashamed of themselves. I turned my head away. I held Lily to me. She was so warm and soft and it was true I have been monumentally lonely. I put the key to the door with eyes barely open, snapped on the lights in the hallway, clambered over the stairs, slumped in a chair in the sitting room.

Eleanor once told me I had a genius for disappointment. Odd the things that stayed with you. I remembered reviving her late one night, it was maybe three and a half years ago, four. I found her out cold in my bed with no clothes on. She wasn't even living here then. I opened and closed the window, called her name, put on her old mix tape in an attempt to wake her tactfully. Knocked loudly on the door. Slammed it. Nothing. I rubbed her sternum and then rubbed and gently scratched above her top lip. There was little in the way of a pulse.

I tried to breathe more life into her while respecting her nakedness, with blankets and bunched sheets, my lips on her lips, dread rising as I called an ambulance. I drew her to her feet, threaded my coat over her, tried to walk her barely conscious body round, bearing her weight over my shoulders, her legs dangling, feet on my feet, like a zombie dancing partner, strands of her hair in my mouth. She weighed almost nothing. I slid pants up her legs and the coat fell off so I tied the bedspread quickly round her, the sharp ribs poking out, no breasts to speak of. I asked the paramedics to look away. I climbed into the ambulance behind her, sat on the blue plastic bench, my arm on the stretcher with all its strappings to hold her – made me think for a second of electric chairs. I kissed each of her eyelids and I tucked my cardigan round her head so there was something soft and warm next to her face, me-smelling, so the skin of her cheeks and neck wouldn't chafe against the thick webbed straps.

The paramedics, two vast men, strong and monosyllabic, were giving her shots of something to revive her, as though they were getting a car engine to spark or start up again mechanically, and all the while I was hoping, praying, barely breathing myself, as though reducing my take-up of air would leave more for her. Gradually a small spread of colour returned to her face. One of her arms lifted itself. After a minute she opened her eyes and motioned for me to leave her with two flicks of her hand. I nodded and swallowed and stood as one well versed in unrequited love scenes knows how to stand, and I peered out of the window but we were fast-moving in the shooting traffic then, and I thought about winching open the door and jumping out neatly, hoping for the best, but instead I apologised, said I'd better stay until we arrived if that was all right with her. She frowned and shrugged and I sat with her a bit more after they gave her a bed, and as she went to sleep I read eighty pages of *Villette* to her.

Then, many hours later, when it was almost dawn and the nurse said she was going to be OK and to come back at lunchtime, I walked all the way home, sat down in the empty flat, not so much heartsore as dismayed out of my brains and strangely affronted that I had to do all this on my own, and then going into school that morning getting ticked off because I was a day late with my reports.

Please.

I ran a bath, elbow-tested it, climbed in holding Lily to me firmly, her legs on my legs, pink dappled sausage-coloured skin and folds of flesh. I patted the slippery creases on the back of her neck. We splashed about in the warm and I washed her hair from behind, the thatch of soft strands so fair it was pale pink, dabbing white foam from her scalp onto my nose. I swivelled her round to see it and she roared with mirth, started waving her hands exuberantly. I sang her sea shanties, my features piratical with grimaces and grins. I turned on the hot tap again, worked up a bank of bubbles in the water. 'Ahoy there, landlubbers,' I called out to the line of shampoo bottles on the lip of the bath. Lily kicked up her legs and began to cackle wildly. She'd have slipped on an eyepatch if she'd had one to hand. Installed a parrot on her shoulder. She was such an easy customer. I kissed her chin. I was almost delirious, as though someone had ladled a gallon of double cream all down me.

'Once a week might be too much for them; once a fortnight then if that's going to be easier for everyone. We can make it work, no problem! Might be better, more achievable. Once a month? We'll just have to see. Give it a go.' Lily's peaceful smile gave me confidence. 'Everybody loves everybody so much, which is the main thing. Few times a year. What everyone wants everyone will have. We'll make it work. We'll make it brilliant.' She screwed up her eyes suddenly; treated my ceaseless ramblings to an indulgent frown. Splashed her fists in the bathwater. 'They can do bedtimes if they want a couple of times a week if they can get organised. Be lovely. I'm not ruling anything out. There's no actual . . . That sound OK?'

Asking permission from a baby! What a pair!

FOUR

There was a slippery glamour to the teenage schoolgirl. Everything was becoming to them: fury, outrage, when they were sullen or sleeping at their desks, blowing smoke rings into the air at the bus stop with concentration, speed-eating hazelnut yoghurt between lessons, boxing up crimson spaghetti sauce in the domestic science lab, ponytail fronds dangling in the Tupperware. Their spots could look quite beautiful from some angles, like defiant punkish jewellery or . . . or geological formations. I loved their determined surges of vitality which made them almost hot to the touch. Even their carelessness could be inspiring; it was a form of bright armour and I tried to be respectful towards it when I didn't meet it head on. (No homework, for example, and no interesting excuses – that was tiresome.)

What ailed adolescent girls was an acknowledged aspect of my job alongside what might lift the ailing. They called me Mum sometimes, the younger ones, and they gasped with horror as though no one had done it before. (I did it myself.) But the things I learned at school did not work at home.

I could only think blood relations had different requirements of each other. The rate of exchange wasn't the same. The economy of sympathy had a different cellular structure. I had the wrong kind of patience, the wrong kind of sentimentality as far as Eleanor was concerned. The wrong arms and legs and eyes and ears and—

At home, the failures piling up were excoriating. I could neither understand nor believe the things I saw. Jean could tell I was suffering. 'Don't try so hard,' she warned me. 'Louisa couldn't stand me for years. I just gave her a wide berth. Don't take everything so personally. It just takes time.' That gave me confidence and I made up my mind to admire Eleanor from afar. I would not let her burn away at me so fiercely and I was friendly and impersonal while I got some of my strength back. I tried to let her bounce off me, but the smashes of loathing that came from her, the poisoned silence, the lying and hostility and stealing and recriminations that followed, as though I had taken *her* things, I wasn't up to it. She'd tell it differently, of course, but she wouldn't talk to me. The pain of cohabiting with someone who despised you, who thought you quite a few rungs lower than human. Bracing, that. A particular species of domestic violence.

It started a few weeks after she hit thirteen. The way she swung her love away from me. I who had been father and mother to her, bed, table and chair, and then when our ordinary smiling exchanges turned to derision and cruelty it did feel like small acts of murder coming my way. I lost my nerve. I couldn't be civil to myself. There was no home at home. One awful night I locked myself in the bathroom and punched myself in the face. I couldn't think what else to do. I heard a deep ringing sound and sat for a few moments on the edge of the bath, stroking my hot cheekbone. I was shocked to find I was in a world where there was nothing soft for me, no welcome. Her terrible attempts to black me out. There was no anything. One morning I read a thing in the paper about trauma and its causes and treatments. The journalist was saying that the really damaging thing about the assault she experienced as a teenager was the knowledge that she was absolutely nothing in the other person's eyes.

Shy and sweet to me at twelve, doting almost, she started staying out all night when she wasn't quite fourteen: 'It's impossible for me to breathe when I'm with you.' I drove round in my little car with the night owls and the kerb crawlers. I stopped outside late-closing pubs and her friends' tall, judgemental houses. I was like a Victorian infant trying to track down its errant father. Sometimes the mothers took pity on me. 'What's wrong with that woman?' the husbands said. Once I yanked her out of someone's bed into the street with her screeching at me and pulling my hair, my heart pummelling as though I was the thief. I was at sea with her and without her, out of my depth, famished, debased and drowning so it was odd to be hailed at school as a champion of the suffering teen. It's not unusual to lead a double life, certainly, but it was a bit grotesque to be quite so good at things and quite so bad.

On Thursdays they traipsed in to see me at four o'clock – the unhappy hour – when the smell of floor polish was always at its strongest, its sourest; I think the heating triggered it towards the end of the day. She might be fifteen, mottled with anxiety, something of a wire coat hanger to her general atmosphere, bringing to my already heaving desk sharp nervous responsibilities. She could be twelve and generously carefree, a loose-knit frankness to her spirit, home-made jumper, practical swimmer's build, bronzed and peeling at the nose from a weekend's childish playing in the sunshine, only she was worried now about her best friend who wasn't the same after the holidays – 'She maybe doesn't like me any more?' Or seventeen, high-shouldered and tearful after a botched exam or stricken from a ruinous boy situation (she wouldn't divulge but she might hint). I tried to organise my sympathy so it wasn't prying.

Once, a Year 11 girl asked me if I would go with her to the doctor's. She came to the staff room at lunchtime, handling herself so carefully I thought of the fingers of china figurines. I wiped cream of mushroom soup from the corners of my mouth and took her to a side room, gave her my untouched mug of coffee, which was borderline illegal, gently closing the door with the edge of my shoe. I sat, smiled, waited. I apologised for the torturous recorder practice coming from the music room, swearing to make her feel comfortable, that we were grown-ups together. She was clever, measured, cold. She had a certain glossy sharpness of tone, which gave me the impression, before we began, that there were things I could say that would constitute grave errors. She did that thing I don't love which is bringing aspects of life more properly belonging to business transactions into a personal arena. Still. People had to cling on to a bit of bravado in hard times, even if it wasn't to my taste. (Jean said God in *Paradise Lost* often spoke a dreary legalese.)

'Are you telling me to keep what you say completely secret? I can do that as long as I don't consider you or any other persons to be at risk.'

'But how would you know?'

'You'll just have to trust me. All right?'

I wished I was Jean with her flair for certainty, her firm shelf of bosom. It was obviously a pregnancy, I thought, and it was, ten weeks already – late in the day.

I noticed she didn't have a single fingernail remaining and yet she told me proudly she had not fallen behind with her work. We discussed the implications for three solid lunch hours. 'Ships in the night, miss,' was all she said about the other party – quite impressive for sixteen. When you lived a life that didn't include being touched, that kind of intimacy was potent.

'I could have the baby,' she said. 'My mum would take over, because that's what she does, so I'd get my life back pretty fast.'

'When I was pregnant with my daughter, the father wasn't very ... ' I didn't tell him until after she was born. His chief concern was for his privacy.

'Sorry, miss, I don't want to get distracted.'

In the end she gave me her word she would tell her mother. I had lightly pressed for that course of action all along. 'Chapeau!' Jean said. (I did not name the girl, nor confirm the name when she guessed correctly.) 'I'd have made sandwiches and gone with her to the clinic. We'd have sung "We Shall Overcome" on the way. "Nellie the Elephant", maybe. Had a stiff gin afterwards and I would probably have been struck off or something, condemned to supervising the detention class for all eternity.' (Detention was enjoying a sudden spike in popularity since the recent launch of 'detention baguettes', which came in cheese, ham, and cheese and ham.) We were both laughing and I couldn't help myself: 'You'd have made a legendary back-street abortionist, Jean.'

She bowed.

Sometimes we got a girl coming to us with existential misgivings, fearful that she felt much more than she could shoulder, that *she* was too much, or she wanted too much from life – or it from her. Before you knew it, you felt along the lines of similar experience in yourself, and if you pressed down on the feeling like a patch of two-day-old bruising, mauve and lemon, the pair of you became for a moment almost twins. Competitive notes crept in sometimes that you couldn't exactly be proud of. You might envy her her sense of freedom, the way she moved her arms, long and narrow as iris leaves, as though there was all the space in the world for them. How did she learn to feel that way about herself? You could even envy her having a *you* to hear her out. At a conference Jean once heard another teacher say, 'You can only be as happy as your most unhappy pupil.'

'I loathe that kind of talk,' she said.

The girls at school were obsessed with food, and Jean and I often discussed it. 'We ought to write a book about eating disorders and put our feet up and watch the money roll in,' she said.

'We *could* . . .' I floundered slightly. I knew it wasn't generally considered a subject with a jackpot attached.

For some of the girls, food was the bitter enemy. They were at war with life and it was the closest battle to hand. 'If you can't feel at peace in your own body, your chances of being happy in yourself are just about zero,' I said to Jean.

She was less forgiving. She saw self-indulgence in self-denial, vanity, weakness of character. 'They shouldn't mind about being thin so much. It's shallow and boring. It's beneath us all.' There was a fashion in Year 9 for eating an entire raw cabbage in the evening. Some of the sixth-form girls were planning a trip to India in the hope of contracting amoebic dysentery. That made me sad. 'It's a dangerous attempt to comfort the self more than anything else, the not eating; a reaction to intolerable circumstances, a coping strategy that misfires badly. It's a sort of tyranny.'

'If you say so.' Jean looked doubtful.

There was a three-month period when Eleanor used to come

home from school and be sick into a carrier in her bedroom. I would retrieve it every night after she had fallen asleep and take it outside to the bins. It was a dreadful way to end the day. Humans had such monstrous ways of consoling themselves.

Things were very raw in the here and now. The last two times Eleanor came round she left within half an hour. Lily's second birthday she ignored entirely. Everything I did was a mistake. I tried not to let extremes enter any of my behaviour, but it was clear my forced mildness had its own power to offend. I wished she would hand me a script, a set of instructions, what to say what to do what to feel. Keeping Lily here might have meant Eleanor clinging to me – but no.

Sometimes I thought the more Eleanor evaded and erased me the more I needed her. There were sharp ambushes when her absence hit me sternly. When I heard torch songs on the car radio – anthems about the seamy side of love, its injustices, mis-understandings, betrayals, the endless waiting – I often pictured her not thinking about me. Neglect your children and they will be obsessed with you for life – I read that once – but what about when they neglected you?

I imagined kidnapping her to the wilds of Scotland, each of my children hoisted on a hip, muscles flexed, in our damp waterproofs, to that last bit of wilderness in the United Kingdom, it was meant to be beautiful, catching pike and roasting it on a bonfire, spitting the bones. Lil and I could keep her safe. I pictured that expanse of wilderness sometimes, riddled with addicts in their slack des-peration, sick-with-worry mothers behind every tree, each wall of bracken. Cascades of hope, cascades of despair. I dreamed I took her to Lourdes one summer, watched her stand uncertainly and throw down her crutches, which splintered into matchsticks on the steps. I picked a few up, stowed them in my pocket to keep as souvenirs. They probably had dealers there now anyway.

I breathed my love onto Lily. What we felt for each other had a lot of heat and urgency. I was strong but I was careful. I teaspooned love into her. People didn't speak much of the thick currents of emotion that flowed between the single parent and the only child, the joint unbridled purpose, the coming first with each other, the aims shared, doubled, twinned. The thick swoon of it. It had been the same with Eleanor when she was little. No dilution, everything directly beamed heat and light. Synchronised breathing, warm tessellated limbs. I sometimes thought the politicians who lambasted single parents for their irresponsibility, their sexual assault on the fabric of society, were just consumed with jealousy that two people could be so close. What did they know?

I liked to chat to Lily in the car when she was sleeping. In the rear-view mirror I stared at the smooth half-moons of her eyelids. 'Thing is, they can be really brilliant, but quite a lot of the time they're just not doing so well.' For a bedtime story it wasn't exactly— She woke and squealed suddenly, high-pitched, high-spirited, still it felt like intervention: ENOUGH!

I lifted her out of the car, set her on the pavement in her red buckled shoes and cream ribbed tights, unlocked the door, snapped on the lights in the hallway, kissed her cheeks. She sat opposite me in the bath these days, so grown up. 'Look. We'll see if they can come round on Sunday for a roast dinner. You can help me make jam tarts. How about that?'

I wanted Eleanor and me to be like divorced parents. Co-mothering – I started to use that term. I so missed having my own mother to discuss Eleanor with when she was little. To raise a child as a collaboration must be astonishing. My friends who still had men in their lives said, Oh do give it a rest, you don't know what you're on about, but I didn't believe them.

If Eleanor had an all-consuming job I would have lent a hand to the best of my ability. We would have discussed Lil in the evenings when she came in from work, her latest sayings, her expanding library of tricks. And 'You'll never GUESS what happened then!' I'd smile, handing her a drink or an onion on a board to chop, and Eleanor so eager to know all the details of her waking hours, the facts and footnotes and the marginalia.

Those first few weeks when I started at college, I could scarcely believe it was finally happening. I sat on the top of the 29, willing the bus forward, 'Come on! Come on!' I couldn't wait to get home and tell my mother everything. 'Slow down! Slow down!' she said to me. 'You're going ninety miles an hour. I can't bear to miss a single thing.' We were so happy! And then when I got my first job at school and I had a form with my name on (a form of one's own!), she wanted to know all about the girls. What they wanted to be when they grew up, how they did their hair, where they would ideally go for their holidays, if they could go anywhere.

The way Eleanor lived *was* all-consuming, anyway. The structure of her days. There was something so searing in young people whose bearing strongly brought to mind the end of life.

I made up my mind to wean myself off Eleanor. Remove myself from the fray and bow out. Call on all available devices of detachment. I had to graft myself to something more sustaining even if just for appearances' sake. Two people couldn't go down. Three. It was right to concentrate on Lily now. I couldn't keep trying to come up with new things in myself. Hard to say you were giving up exactly when there were no longer things you could reasonably expect. In a couple of years Eleanor would be thirty! I would keep her hazy shape in view, though. I'd hold her close to me in theory as one holds a new baby in the crook of one's arm before it is born, or the memory of a person who has recently died and you are not quite sure who is comforting whom or who can see and who is blind. It would take sleight of hand not to look at things head on, but instead to soften my ideas around her, let them be lacy at their edges and fall away. I couldn't keep on trying to balance the equations all the time. That my care had equalled what she was living.

FIVE

I started to regret the nature of our street. We had the top flat in a house, two floors – well, one and a half – and they were good houses, dark London brick with bay windows, solid with fireplaces and floorboards, in a long terrace that was mostly Caribbean and Cypriot and Irish families – a lot of little children in beautiful clothes on Sunday mornings – but we were ten minutes from a large thoroughfare notorious for prostitution, and in the last few years the trade had seeped onto our street. It used to be that on Fridays and Saturdays there were a couple of girls standing on the corners from about four thirty, but it was most days now and some were young. They looked impassive in their scant skirts or thin leggings, pale-lipped, goosebumps, raw bare limbs. I dreaded walking home. I found it hard to handle myself. Sometimes they wore white blouses with open-necked collars that could have been part of their school uniforms. There were often kerb crawlers, the pressure of the cars' slow roar threatening your walking, a rush of engine smoke in your throat, nasty glances mocking your careful steps, and they would say things like 'Jump in, love' if they were of good cheer or sometimes just 'Get in' or 'How much?' even though there was a set rate.

It happened to me, it happened to Eleanor.

'They're just sad old gits, I feel sorry for them.'

'I don't,' she said.

In the main we travelled to and from school together and when she went out with her friends I met her from the bus stop until she was quite old, thirteen or fourteen, when she didn't want me any more. Slammed doors, bitter recriminations, four-day punishment silences. 'Just keep walking,' I said to her. 'Don't stop or anything, just quicken your pace slightly and if you keep yourself to yourself and don't make eye contact they'll soon get the message. Make sure your hair is tied back and your coat is done up. Put the collar up, that's right. Head down.' It's hard to believe we ever had such conversations. My mother talked to me a great deal about the sensible precautions to take against the opposite sex, 'men being what they are'. I saw great lines of them with threats and fists who needed to be soothed and flattered. I thought of men and women as pestle and mortar then.

One afternoon a car hovered alongside me as I was pushing Lily in her buggy. I felt the sharp flood of exhaust fumes in my mouth and nose. She was three and a bit now, Paddington-ish in the old duffel coat Sarah had found us, and she could walk for a mile, no trouble, but when tired she would climb into her pushchair for an easy life. We were reminiscing about when she was a baby. The capacity of a three-year-old to dwell on her youthful exploits with fond nostalgia! 'When I was little I said "da" for thank you,' she reminded me. She widened her eyes and hooped her mouth comically, as if to say can you *even*. We were both giggling.

The car pulled over. 'Hop in,' the driver said. He was sixtyish, pasty, bald, sneering.

I stared at him. 'Are you out of your mind? I'm taking my granddaughter to the swings.'

'She can sit up front.'

My mouth opened and closed on unformed words, the whole street blazing and the man now smirking at me. I staggered slightly, boiling rage red on my skin, and if I hadn't had the pram to prop me up I might have gone over. I must have done something truly ugly with my face then, because suddenly he was screeching at me. Mad swear words that didn't go together. 'Fuck you sad bitch shit cunt.' His voice livid gunfire boring into me.

I heard myself apologise. I was afraid.

'Don't flatter yourself, love,' the man called after me and I laughed nervously and kept on walking at speed, which he must have taken as a further slight because he drove up the street and levelled with me and spat at me through the window and a little gobbet of his white phlegm landed on my tights, just above the ankle bone.

I went home in a daze, tore off my tights, soaped my legs until they were crimson. A few new bluish veins zigzagged down the inside of my feet to torment me. My knees looked cobbled in a way I didn't recognise. I set Lily on my lap and we watched antique cartoons all afternoon – *Dastardly and Muttley, Hong Kong Phooey*, 'number one super guy' (I always liked him) – mocked by the bright sunshine we were squandering. I felt points of shame all over my body. The colourful characters flashed bright onto Lily's skin, dancing wildly in her eyes. I had that cold sensation you can get when you have lied to yourself.

Three months later we moved to a smaller flat – just over half the size, one bed – on the top floor of a house in a better road half a mile away. A street with a little Methodist church at one end with dance classes and gymnastics and a small garden where children played out after school. I should have done it years ago.

Under our new roof I was a bit revitalised, the shadows of life lifting and a fresh, clearer light over things when the world had been overcast for so long. I got us a cheap package deal to Majorca, five days stretched out on the sand and on our balcony, the air very soft, pink-layered evening skies, low quilted heat. We larked about in the shallows, laughing and shrieking, then on the third day I taught Lily breaststroke, supporting her frame from underneath as she cut semicircles in the sea with her tanned arms. We played cards and pinball machines in the blue hotel bar in the late afternoon, wrote postcards to Eleanor, sharing a fizzy orange drink, drawing in our sketchbooks in the evenings on our little balcony scented with suncream and the sea and Lily's warm salty skin and scorched grasses and wax crayons and night-flowering jasmine. One lunchtime we got chips from a café called Tea like Mummy Makes and ate them standing in the peacock-coloured sea, Lily's gold hair streaming back towards me in the hot wind like a siren. The colours and the heat and the smell of everything – I knew I would never forget. She begged and begged me to buy her a stout lemon-yellow towelling bikini in the market, and I gave in. It was the first thing she'd ever asked me for, I realised. She was mad with pleasure afterwards. Couldn't *believe* it.

On the last night the hotel had a beauty contest with a swimsuit parade, which was tiresome, but after that each of the competitors had to sew a patch onto a man's jeans while he was still wearing them. The men stood in a row like some kind of identity parade, entirely still, with great mock frowns on their faces, wincing or pretending to as the women, in evening dresses now, bobbed and bent and stitched on stage. It was beginning to get dark but still the heat hung thickly. Lily watched transfixed. We couldn't see the needles or the thread from our seats, so the women looked as though they were performing some symbolic ceremonial rite or worship relating to bums. I had the sense she felt she was witnessing something essential and eternal about how things lay between women and men. She had a wedge of chocolate gateau with glossy scalloped icing from the last-night buffet and she forked in small mouthfuls without looking at it at all, occasionally dabbing at the corners of her mouth, completely riveted until she was suddenly asleep in my arms. I sat there holding her as the hotel guests grew wilder and more raucous, and as she relaxed into me it was as though we were the same person.

In the eighteen months that followed, there was a new buoyancy. Lily and I were winning. I loosened myself. My cheeks stopped burning. I looked forward to mornings especially now, the two of us bleary-eyed at the kitchen table, competing to see who could put away the most toast. The mad celebrations afforded by ordinary time when cascades of cornflakes actually made me think of autumn leaves! Pencil cases and hairbrushes mixed easily with jam pots. Piles of plimsolls by the door. It was so civilised. I dropped Lily off at the infants' school on my way into work, scooped her at the end of the day from the late club at half four. The evenings settled on us gently and we read our books side by side on the sofa, a saucer of biscuits balanced on a cushion, until six, when we put the television on. At seven we ate, then I got down to my marking.

She set all our routines. On the first Friday of the month we should share a cream bun, she said – a Napoleon, iced white with a brown feathered decoration, or a strawberry tart with a ring of granular piped cream framing the glazed fruit, or meringues sandwiched together with sweetened cream, fragile in their skirts of pleated paper. Spaghetti and tomato sauce on Monday nights, please. (She liked to 'chip up the onion'.) A tin of Fanta on Sunday afternoons after gymnastics. I said yes to everything. To have a child who didn't punish me through food . . . She had such a sense of occasion. Every Saturday morning she came into the bedroom carrying plates of toast and jam and the hem of her nightie. 'Breakfast's on, Ru!' She was weaving nets of expectation and affection. Crumbs and giggling in the tangled bedclothes. I didn't need anything else. It was like being God or the Queen. The luxurious sensation as I arranged myself next to her in the cool sheets at night, taking care not to wake her, the quiet joy almost inexpressible. I was a professional gambler on a lucky streak. I loved the simple rubbing-along with another person, friendliness, a calm and busy rhythm, lustre and life cheer, snippets of shared news, flapjacks with raisins (she loved raisins), our stupid jokes.

Customer: 'Why does that cake there cost more than that cake over there?'

Shopkeeper: 'That cake there?'

Customer: 'Yes, that cake there.'

Shopkeeper: 'That's Madeira cake.'

It didn't take much to make you laugh when you were smiling your head off anyway.

She was very organised for a person of five, her faith in the two of us touching and complete. She organised me. The alienation in my veins started defrosting, the shock and dread loosening its hold after decades. Since I was her age, to speak honestly for a moment, if I could afford that now.

Very gently I relaxed myself. It felt as though I had recovered from a disease. Another year passed without blame or injury. Convalescence, the end of convalescence, the bit that came after when a day with a small mouth ulcer rubbing against the ridge of a tooth counted as a terrible day. It wasn't a life in the shadows any more – instead exhilaration, free-running cheer that had no basis of anxiety. Hope, I suppose it was. The sky looked huge. The world felt promising and clear. I smoothed the sheets each morning as though for the limbs of a heroic guest. I spent days in a row with courage intact so that if someone was rude to me in a shop I could be witty or defiant, instead of almost jumping through the window. Aches I had put down to age vanished from my shoulders and my villainous knee. I had wild rushes of high spirits that lasted for weeks. It was the closest I had come to a honeymoon possibly. At school my lessons were greatly improved. The girls were intrigued. 'Miss, are you *actually*?' Our conversations grew increasingly rich and wild. 'The best poets faced the full range of their experience with their full intelligence. What would it feel like to do this to ourselves?' At night I could sleep seven hours straight without trying, without failing. One lunchtime I slipped on some orange juice in the dining hall and went over and a chain of near-instant bruises sprung up across my shin, and I laughed at myself for the first time in my life.

I still mourned Eleanor, now and then, in the late afternoons particularly when it was beginning to get dark and I was high on tea. It was a quiet voice now, discreet and low-key when for years it had been deafening. It didn't try to do me in. I had accepted things about myself. She knew I was here if she needed anything, everything. I would no longer allow myself to feel pilloried by the lack of her. I let go of her hands. I stopped hating the night. Instead, I surrounded myself with the idea of bad things *not* happening; although occasionally I woke and prayed she wouldn't smash into oncoming traffic.

I had a drink that spring with Christine, Fran and Sarah. 'Here we all are again,' one of us said, without much zeal, might have been me. It was a grim evening, the weather atrocious – spiteful almost – but I suddenly remembered I had a bottle of crème de cassis a grateful parent had given at Christmas, so I mixed a little for each of us with cold white wine that Sarah brought. I handed out the glasses proudly, the liquid a strong, deep pink like those large bottles they used to have in the windows of pharmacies. Christine had sheer black tights with little polka dots. I complimented her and she gave a sharp little bark-like laugh. That night Eleanor went entirely unmentioned between us. I only noticed after they had gone. Just as they were leaving, Sarah murmured, 'And things with you are generally, would you say . . . ?' and I just told her, 'All is well.'

I loved the mad proportions of her grin.

Jean and I began to telephone each other regularly, the two of us still sailing along in the creaky old boat piled high with ancient textbooks, scalloped pencil sharpenings, blackboard wipers; a vessel brimming with the brightness of teenage girl brain, wildly oversensitive and callous as they could be, appallingly spelt and coffee-stained and fag-scented, with clumps of Rimmel's Hide the Blemish on their cardigans and flakes of ancient (and illegal) Tippex snowing from the pages of their exercise books. Wise captains, were we? Possibly.

And then one evening her strong hurt voice on the telephone: 'Alan's gone, it's for good this time.' I dropped Lily at her friend's and went on to Jean's with a jug of daffodils. 'He isn't a good person but he's family,' she said. She took a raspberry Swiss roll from the cupboard, unwrapped it, cut it briskly into six, the spirals of red jam and white synthetic cream glowing like gashes and their ointment. I had only met him a few times and remembered his atmosphere of leap and lunge, like you might associate with a large playful dog.

It had always been the spring when she'd discovered his affairs.

Towards the end of the evening she tried out a few thoughts on me. Jean being Jean they were delivered with great emphasis, but I knew from knowing her for so long that they represented new lines of enquiry. The secret in life, she now *knew*, was not to be debased by any poor treatment that might come your way. It was not easy, certainly, but the secret was to think, 'How very *odd*'; to be puzzled, annoyed possibly, unimpressed of course, better yet *un-thrilled* (that was her word of the week), but not to let it degrade you. 'You can't allow the past to make your present appear dubious. It's perhaps an artistic problem, as much as anything else, how to live.' Jean had gone very Bloomsbury Group of late. Alan's behaviour was mean-spirited and self-serving, she had decided. 'But I can't let that define me. I won't.' She held up her hands as though someone were about to shoot. 'I'm not guilty, Ruth.'

I nodded.

Her doctor suggested a course of antidepressants. 'It's something she says every couple of years. But I always think much better not. And then, ages ago, someone told me it makes your car insurance rocket, so that put me right off, although, as you know, I never learnt to drive. I suppose I'm more a cup of tea and a sit-down, get into bed with a good book kind of grin and bear it, gin and bear it person, two glasses of wine and a Camembert eaten straight from the box with a spoon when the chips are down. Not that I'm against pills. I just see them as a last resort. Something like that. Fine for others but not quite for me. Like bridge, perhaps. Or the tango.'

'Fair enough.' I was laughing at the thought of the gin and the chips and the Camembert in bed. Jean liked people to know she thought the Continent very superior when it came to sophistication, attitudes towards sex in literature, philosophy, TV snacks, etc. Her salads were thatched with croutons and lardons.

'And then I always felt Alan would be winning if I had to medicate myself to put up with his crap. No, no, no. And why is it women are pushed towards self-improvement schemes when what's required is structural change? I don't buy it. Spritz your sadness with Chanel No. 5? Stuff your cushions with superfluous body hair? I used to think like that when I was young, but not now. It's all lies. And now Louisa's weighed in. Could have done without that. I need more resilience, apparently. "You know what Dad's like." So I said, I think resilience as a word is morally bankrupt. It's what people require of you when they don't intend to treat you very well. She didn't like that. Oh dear! I'm going to take her youngest to *As You Like It* at half-term. Might have to stuff her with sweeties to keep her awake. Doesn't matter if she has a kip anyway. What were we saying? Oh yes, antidepressants.'

How could you not love Jean?

Eleanor visited rarely now. We went down from every two months to every three, then as-and-when. Planned spontaneity. When I felt bold, I'd ring her and say in a voice that was softened but not sweetened (that maddened her): 'We'd love to see you.'

I made food for her on the rare occasions that she did come, a Sunday dinner at four for three. It was when Jane Austen's people would have dined, not that we were very bonnety in Finsbury Park. We put out a red-and-white-checked tablecloth for her, a few flowers in a jug. I wanted more the ease and welcome of a seaside B&B than something befitting a hallowed foreign dignitary. Jean came back from the National Gallery saying, 'No one does checked tablecloths like Pierre Bonnard.' I showed Eleanor and Lily the postcard she'd bought me. Jean knew I couldn't flit around London with the same kind of ease. She was a good friend. The way she didn't ask me things was so respectful.

The extreme satisfaction of getting a bit of food down Eleanor when she did show up. She had long ago lost the art of the mechanics of eating, the simple up-down of knife and fork; her body sharp and empty as if she had no hospitality to offer herself. She looked harder now in her face, but the suggestion of things being ill-aligned made her presence more affecting, if anything, with its nervous brittleness and tensions. Her eyes had gathered information relating to sorrow, relating to hardship, that her broad full mouth denied. She dared you to ask anything, to think anything, to feel anything. There was a sort of lurking threat suspended in the air for anyone who broke her commands. Sharp jarring currents of vulnerability and contempt. Maybe that was only if you were her mum. But occasionally there were moments when she seemed beseeching. I felt she needed a bit of admiration now. Still I never understood why her eating filled *me* up.

I sometimes sat in the bedroom leaving the girls at the table in the front room, facing away from the door to give them their privacy. They seemed like sisters at these moments, Eleanor very much top dog. Lily was smaller in her mother's presence than at any other time, her hands placed serenely on her lap under the table. She was more careful, too careful, watchful and still. One afternoon I brought them in some quartered oranges and told them silly stories about the girls at school; the howlers people had written in their mock exams. 'Jane Eyre should have made an effort to be funner with her cousins and not just hide away with a book the whole time which was very rude and judgemental to be honest.'

Eleanor protested. 'You mustn't tell us these things!' She was shocked at my indiscretion. About some things she had very high standards. There was a sense I got that some strand of purity in her could only see impurity in me. Part of her power to intimidate had always come from the way she looked, I think. Beauty was tied up with respect and integrity – truth, I suppose – via nature, something like that, anyway. Perhaps it was the fact that it was almost impossible to say no to someone with that kind of full visual charge because you couldn't help feeling they were the ones who should be saying no to you.

Lily got taller, cleverer, sweeter, bigger, stronger, that was her job. Nothing about her made you think of incubators now. I would do her a disservice to remember such things. We had a weekend in Brighton. It was an ancient train; the carriage still had old-fashioned compartments defined by mahogany doors with springy string mesh luggage racks overhead. We had one to ourselves. Lily slipped her shoes off and lay down fully extended. I did the same on the opposite bench, the dry prickle of the chequered carriage cloth against my bare legs. Out of the window of this mad travelling dormitory, flashes of red terraces and smooth quilts of green.

When we reached the beach, Lily covered me completely in stones with only my eyes showing – it was so cool and peaceful under there. I felt a small child slip out of me and bolt into the sea! I dried her in my cardigan, blotting her with the skirts of my dress. The sky clouded over. I put the picnic blanket round her shoulders to make a shawl, the fringes bouncing off her knees as we walked back to the guest house. You look like a fortune-teller, I said. We played rummy for Minstrels in the tea room at the Pavilion, eating our winnings surreptitiously. The hem on the waitress's black skirt was coming down in bulky lumps. Her boss ticked her off about it and we pulled faces behind his back to make her smile. From the window of the B&B we could see amazing coral-coloured poppies zigzag in a line that followed a broken fence.

We chatted at bedtime as she slipped into sleep. 'Your mum and I went to Paris once. Was so lovely. We stayed at the Hotel Amelot, which was famous for being the cheapest nice hotel. It was a hundred francs a night for a twin but the chambermaid said if we just used one bed it would be eighty-nine, so we did that. It was next to the Winter Circus and we went one night and it was amazing with sea lions clapping and chorus girls in red silk top hats standing up on galloping horses. And there was an orchestra above the circus ring with real violinists and the men clowns had white court shoes with a little heel. We were so happy!'

We wandered back to the station in the lightest of showers the next day. I loved seeing raindrops in people's hair. I was still finding things out about myself – that pleased me. It was too early to say whether Lily would have her mother's looks. Her eyes were a deep, frank dark grey-blue, like the metal-coloured sea, hazy and undefined.

SIX

We only saw Eleanor a handful of times during the next three years. On each occasion she was a little more reduced. She no longer looked at me with defiance and those jets of fury; there was a mild bewilderment to her and hardly any harshness at all. We were in a different phase. Her atmosphere was entirely sad. There was the sense of an ending. I gave her small amounts of money, although she didn't ask. In return she let me hug her, the body between my arms so slight my elbows almost touched. I noticed after her visits that there were a few things missing. I should have minded but I didn't somehow. It felt like she was borrowing life rafts. I liked to give her a painting or drawing of Lily's to take home with her and she managed to react as though this was a great honour, which meant more in its way than the clock radio or the camera going.

'Hey, I know, why not crash here for a couple of days?' I offered at the door. It was a sort of joke between us now. She grinned a wonky sheepish grin. Once she even said, 'Oh Mum!' as if I had left the house without my trousers, cheated in a game of snakes and ladders, and I smiled the smile of the defeated. After she went

I noticed she had taken all the plasters from the medical box which felt a bit cruel to her own child's scuffed knees and paper cuts, but I just bought more. And possibly your daughters had an inalienable right to your medical supplies for life. I didn't know what other people would think. I didn't care.

The last time she was here, in the spring, we all sat outside on the front steps with ice-cold tins of Fanta I'd bought specially, a few cherries sunning themselves in a pale green dish at our feet. Lily had her drawing things spread out around her and was working on a picture of the terraced houses opposite. It was very peaceful: just the sound of her soft B pencil sketching and our breaths and snatches of birdsong. Eleanor had been quiet for a while and I thought she was asleep, but then she stirred herself and began to look intently at the drawing. 'The way you've done the bricks!' she said, her voice thin and scratchy from waking, still held kindness and there were odd flecks of excitement in her eyes. 'Not all of them but just enough to tell us that the whole thing is made of brick. You're brilliant!' Lily smiled and shrugged. I was amazed that someone who could barely function was able to be so generous. It was a bit heroic and romantic, yes. There was still some *her* there. I felt proud and hoped it might do her good, seeing that in my eyes. That it would bolster her, even though she did look bad, her teeth were bad now, her eyes were bad, tight-looking, bird-like, witchy. I knew she couldn't keep any aspect of herself up for very long.

I was trying to think what she needed from us as we sat there. Hard to know how to give to people who only wanted what would mutilate. But she ate with us, really ate for the first time, that afternoon. She was ravenous, concentrating. Sweet things particularly. I wondered if we were the only time she did eat. Three meals a year. Later that afternoon the girls did a beautiful painting of a horse, Lily the front half and Eleanor the rear, like pantomime people. The splayed legs caused much mirth. They let me do the tail. If Eleanor's teeth were bad, her arms were very bad – they looked furious – but she wasn't angry with me. It made all the difference. We could be soft with each other if there was going to be some sympathy. She caught me gazing at her face and smiling foolishly to the brim because I was so happy to have her close by and couldn't help myself from showing it, and she looked up and smiled also.

'Could you face coming to the dentist?' I asked. 'If I make an appointment. Just to check everything's ... won't take half an hour.'

She shook her head, lowered her eyes. 'But thanks.'

I could hear more sensible people laughing in my face, but there was some proper closeness and trust finally. Later that evening she nodded out on the sofa and I put a blanket over her and Lily fell asleep too at her side, and it made me think of the way you sleep while your baby is sleeping at the start of things, the ecstasy when she finally does sleep and you feel so jubilant you almost wake her up to celebrate! I slipped in next to Lily on the sofa and before I knew it all three of us were conked out in a row – that was a first – and as I drifted off, the phrase *three-headed monster* came to me. When I woke, she was gone. I'd left a few notes out on the table just in case, not much. I didn't know what her life was like now; whether she slept in the flat all day or criss-crossed the city accosting strangers, begging for money, scrounging a meal here and there. If an older man was paying for her. It was how I think she often arranged things. Her body she had never valued. Punishment after punishment. The value it had for others made it even more worthless to her, possibly. How you squeezed hope into any of those sentences I did not know.

I once read about a woman who worked in a laboratory that tested beauty products on animals. She said, 'The way you deal with it is you disassociate yourself from that animal. You don't let it get to you. You put up that barrier.' That was what Eleanor did. She did it with herself.

Her flat was in my name, or it would have been long gone. I bought it with money her father gave me when she was a baby, rented it out until she needed somewhere. That sort of thing was usual now, maintenance and child support, but it was scarcely heard of then. It had all looked so promising – the money and the beautiful little Sickert painting, which had been his grandmother's. But it was a bit horrible the manner in which it was given, the way he looked at me. It took a moment for it to sink in. I had to sign something. Oh. Property wasn't so expensive then. You could get a little flat in London for a few thousand pounds in the early seventies. From what Eleanor said, I gathered it was filled with people now, people coming in dribs and drabs up and down the stairs all through the night. Once she made it sound jolly. Like a sitcom almost. What did I know?

We hadn't seen Ben for a long time. He had never been here, only to the old flat a few times with Eleanor when Lily was tiny, but after that there was a string of reasons why she came on her own, and then when she seemed to stop coming – I don't know what happened. I thought he was better than that, because he had a certain boyish tact or diplomacy and he was clever.

'He didn't like seeing all the prostitutes, Mum.'

'Oh.'

When Lily was six and a half, Ben's mother telephoned, announcing herself by her full name – Barbara Collins King. She spoke grandly to me as though dealing with a guttersnipe from a great height. There was something wrong with the gas fire – a man was coming, but not until next week – and it was sputtering and hiccoughing and farting in the background and I half hoped she might think it was me. I tried to concentrate.

'Ben's going into treatment, result of a court case. Chequebook fraud – nothing serious,' she reassured. The judge had offered prison or a rehabilitation centre paid for by the local authority and – quite amazing this – Ben had chosen the treatment place.

'That's wonderful.' I was thinking of Lily, of course. 'Anything I can do to help, please say.' I was jealous, of course, but I tried to conceal it.

'Eleanor is not to contact him. She's not to telephone, visit or write. If this is to work, he's going to need to make a new life for himself. Change his cast of friends *entirely*. You do understand.' She issued her decrees with barbaric condescension.

'I see.'

'When he gets out, he'll be going to a halfway house for six months, and after that he'll come to me.' She lived near Lewes, I think. Eleanor once said there were tendrils of ivy all over the front of the house, trying their best to suffocate the inmates. 'Do you understand what I am saying to you? Can you give me your word she will stay away?'

Her superior tone piqued my wounded dignity. I was trying to think how Jean would have responded. There would have been an awful lot of fucks. 'Thank you for your clear instructions.' My tone was terse. 'I wish him all the best,' I said. Of course I did. I even wished *her* well in my crabby way. Yet she had never shown the slightest interest in Lily, which I couldn't begin to understand. I read once that sometimes when people's behaviour is very bad it can be because they carry too much sorrow round a given situation. It might be that the fact of Lily made her feel so awful the best thing she felt she could do for her was pretend she did not exist. The kindest thing, if you went in for stark disembodied kindness. Either that or she didn't think Lily was his.

I telephoned Eleanor – unusually, she answered. I told her what Barbara Collins King had said. 'I've not seen him for a while now,' she murmured. 'Good luck to him.'

'Is that a bit sad that you two're out of touch?'

'I don't mind,' she said. 'All he ever wanted to do was sleep.'

'Well that's . . . Well all right then. Be lovely to see you soon. Might you have a Mum-shaped window one of these days?'

She was gone.

I made enquiries about Ben's treatment place; it was a well-known one in Wiltshire. Large Arts and Crafts mansion, Grade II listed, twenty windows to the front elevation. Fashionable, you could say. I rang up for leaflets I already had in a drawer somewhere. It was a masochistic act, I suppose. The brochure showed a garden with vast candy-hued hollyhocks and a blue-grey-painted pavilion. It was £346 a night for the self-paying – more than my weekly wage after tax. I spoke to an out-of-hours admissions person. 'I'm just trying to get a feel of what my friend could expect if she came to you.' My voice was tentative, wary, forlorn – this fantasy was beginning to hurt my own feelings. The man's exasperated sigh wasn't heartening. 'Well, I always tell them on their first evening, listen up: in a year's time a third of you will be clean, a third of you will have relapsed and a third of you will be dead.' He laughed a hollow laugh, stopping abruptly.

I put the phone down. 'Listen up' – what a charlatan.

Four or five months later Lily and I were on the top deck of the bus, at the back, on our way home from the British Museum. It was the last stretch of winter, blazing with sharp skies and light that fell in bars across the plaid velour seats as though inviting us to play a game with counters and dice. In Holborn a few bare branches from passing trees suddenly poked through the windows, dragging and cracking loudly as the bus sped on. We shrieked with laughter and Lily covered our eyes. At Gray's Inn Road a man I was ninety per cent confident was Ben got on and came and sat three rows in front of us, with a huge black and white dog, flat-eared, shaggy, unalert, which spread out in the aisle between the seats. He was with another man, rough-looking, much worse than he was, a demented zeal to his eyes, a laddered scar across his cheek, and this other man was talking wildly. I had the feeling half the passengers were listening. 'At this point the geezer was dying of cancer and he gave this other geezer twenty quid to get Kentucky Fried Chicken for everyone there and the other geezer just fucked off with the money. The food was going to be for him as well as everyone else and he just took the money and he was boasting about it later that night in the pub and I thought, NO. I am not a fan of the geezer who was dying but I can't handle things like that, you have to stand up to a cunt like that. I went for him. I got him and his rucksack flew into the air and I put the boot in too. The geezer's on a hundred tramadol a week and he's calling me a junkie? No. I'm a kind person. I'm not a fighter. But you have to stick up for people sometimes.'

Lily was reading me my favourite book – *Bread and Jam for Frances*. Frances was the little bear who wanted bread and jam for every meal. Her school friend Albert used to have gourmet packed lunches and his mother always gave him black olives and a little cardboard shaker of salt for his celery sticks. I would screw up the bus ticket at this point in the story and she'd unwrap it and we'd pretend to shake salt all over ourselves and Lily would howl with laughter. We were getting close to the end of the book and I could see Ben was scratching his head hard, leaving red welts on the back of his neck, and tiny white flakes were snowing onto his collar. He had always had difficulties holding onto his skin. He was shrunken in his upper body, his ribcage visible through his shirt. He had gone downhill since we last crossed paths, when he had been a bit lavish in his manner, a suggestion that all the world was his sofa. He still had something about him then, some style, streaks of handsome character, the tail end of bravado.

Difficult thoughts came – traces of childhood crashing. The day my father went. She was twenty-five years old and I was, what was I, six? Slipping out to the shops, he said, overdressed for the weather, big coat, hat even; hours passed and she knew he had gone. I thought, he'll be back when he gets hungry, of course he will, and I made busy preparations in my childish landscape, cut the crusts off a sandwich, put out a pint glass, arranged some apple slices on a saucer, watched them duly brown, while she sat frozen in a kitchen chair staring down the facts. After a while she got up, started dusting in the shadows with a look of puzzled concentration. I took care of her after that, we were like a little couple and I brought her tea in bed in the mornings, weak and milky as she liked it. She was a lovely person but even as a child I saw she was young for her age. He had another woman three miles away from us, I heard, and there might have been a boy my age or thereabouts. I didn't know if the rumour was true. Then he left that one and he had a whole other family after that, people said. I didn't know what I was supposed to think. Or perhaps the woman already had children. There might have been another. I knew in any case he was engrossed in his private life. Then I heard he'd got a job at a photographic studio as a commissionaire, with gold rope on his shoulders, greeting the customers as they arrived, ushering them on to gilt chairs in the waiting room where there were mirrors and combs so you could do yourself up for the portraits. Fur coats, necklaces, military uniforms. Family groups.

Once I caught my mother in floods of tears at the kitchen sink and when I asked her what was wrong she said she was crying because she was so happy. None of this was unusual, exactly, but still my childhood required a lot of ingenuity.

He was very restless, was all she told me, searching for words she couldn't find. 'Saw awful things when he was a boy.'

'What sort of things?'

She shook her head. She had the sort of femininity that made harsh feelings impossible.

One evening not long after, a neighbour came and got me from my friend's and said I was to stay at hers. My mother had drunk some disinfectant in the lavatories at Whitechapel station. A guard heard the bottle smash against the tiled floor, found her doubled over in her coat and skirt. Luckily the Royal London was over the road and she was fine after a few days. In some ways she was stronger than before. 'A man gets tired of a woman who sacrifices everything for him,' she told me, sprinkling a little caster sugar on a slice of buttered bread.

I tried ringing a few photographic places from the telephone box by the town hall. I had a list from the phone book and I ticked them off one by one. I didn't want anything from him, just to hear his voice, tell him our news, but he was thin on the ground.

I was like a flasher, in my way, bringing on such scenes.

Lily was shifting uncomfortably on my knees. I tried to neutralise myself. I wanted to tell her something heroic about her dad – and did I say he won all the prizes at his school for physics and maths and everyone said he should be a surgeon? I couldn't bear the idea that she might think him puny. Sometimes I slipped in little things about Eleanor, put in a good word about what a great reader she was, how when she had a book on the go she didn't rest it on a table or a chair or against herself, she held it upright in front of her eyes as though she was interrogating it or on a dinner date. Like the picture of somebody reading.

Just then Ben stood up, and his friend and the dog, and gathered all their stuff and turned round, and as he did so, I felt a tensing of the muscles in Lily's legs and lower back. I sensed the strength of her focus sharpening. I could tell she was about to call out. It was an electric moment. How could she know? Was it his scent? At that moment, she raised her arm and calmly waved, and Ben just smiled and waved back, mildly, not recognising her or me I don't think, but his gesture showed it was in his nature to be cheery to a friendly little stranger. Off he went down the stairs with his pal staggering behind him. I kissed Lily's head. She had gone very still and her stillness frightened me, but then she lifted her palms towards the roof of the bus, as though *she* were the grandma, and pursed her lips like a faithful little fish and then said 'OH OH OH!' and collapsed into giggles. I was so relieved I heard great peals of laughter ringing out of me also.

'We saw your father on the top of a bus one time when we were coming back from the British Museum. He was totally out of it,

I'm afraid, and we'd not seen him for quite a while and he didn't recognise us. But you responded to something in him so tenderly and as he got up to go you just suddenly waved. And do you know what? He smiled and waved right back!' That wasn't a story you could read anyone.

'Your mother and father had an illness that sadly meant they couldn't look after you, so I stepped in, which was not only a privilege but my great pleasure.' That was better. Bit better.

'When you were a baby, I sort of kidnapped you. Just couldn't help myself. You were irresistible. I'd been lonely like you wouldn't believe. The endless evenings ganging up on me.' Shh now, I said to myself. Ridiculous person.

Lily's seventh birthday we were taking seriously. As though in collusion with us, spring sprang daringly early. From our kitchen window a waxy magnolia with cup-shaped flowers rippled purple and white. 'That sky is so blue it's *ridiculous*,' Lily said. In the past, great swathes of frothy cherry blossom have struck me as spiteful beyond belief, but something must have changed, because this year it all looked like birthday decorations. Lily was having a few friends over. Jean and I moved furniture into the bedroom to create more space. She put on bright blue overalls to do it, Pickfords style – 'And heave!' she said theatrically at intervals, sweat trickling off her, plumes of dust. I bought Lily a present from Eleanor, a book of Chinese folk tales with beautiful watercolour illustrations. I pictured Eleanor hovering by the jellies holding Lily's unopened cards up to the light, checking for cash. 'Sorry,' I mouthed to her. 'Mean of me.' Jean gave Lily a long red tin printed with Swiss mountains, full of coloured pencils, forty-eight, aquarelles. It was big of her, especially as she'd recently

confessed that her grandsons, Louisa's eldest two, were only interested in appalling things like rowing and playing the trombone.
The little girl was promising, though.

Lily woke at ten to five on the great day, fizzing exhilarated
anticipation, shouting *happy birthday happy birthday*, kissing the
tight knot in my shoulder, kicking her pink legs up in delight,
pyjamas flapping wildly, until the covers lay all over the floor. It
was more of a finale than an opening scene. I made the bed again
and told her a silly story about a pair of mouse detectives, and we
dozed together for another hour, her breath dissolving against me,
coils of her hair on the pillow like jewellery. She laughed a little in
her dreams, the heat coming off her concentrated and luxurious.
I knew she would need her own bed soon, but we weren't there
yet. Not quite.

I had promised her a sausage in a bun with a birthday candle
and a fried egg with frilly edges, and when she woke a second time
I tied a striped apron over my nightie and started frying right away.
The pan smoked and spat and I opened the window to let the day
in. The morning was sparkling, the light sharp and silvery over the
street. The violin (quarter-size) I had bought her from a small ad in
the local paper (£19.99) lay wrapped up on the table in yellow paper.
There was so much sunshine that we took our breakfast and ate it
sitting on cushions on the front step, watching the world go by in
the fashion of Greek widows. Christine had dropped an elaborate
dragon-shaped stunt kite round the day before, and we opened it
together, although we couldn't understand it. Sarah had found her
an old dress, blue and white chevron pattern, V neck, puff sleeves,
real silk, 1930s; she'd shortened it, taken it in, added a frill at the
hem, and after breakfast Lily stepped into it and I buttoned her up
and tied the sash in a bow, tugged and plumped the gathers in the

sleeves. She walked round the flat holding the full skirt out in her right hand, her other hand on her hip, the crisp silk rustling, pointing her toes as she stepped as though searching for a clearing in an enchanted wood. She was suddenly a Disney version of my mother. 'Never going to take it off,' she cooed, her voice a slip of blue ribbon.

I remembered sitting next to my mother then, the warm animal comfort of it, being at her side with our thighs touching so you couldn't really tell whose leg was yours. Two people with one pulse. She liked to sew in the evenings and she sometimes asked me to thread her needles or run and fetch embroidery wool or pins from the cupboard upstairs, and I always ran as fast as I could. She taught herself to do smocking from a Victorian manual and French seams and invisible mending. It was very like her that one of the things she did best had a realm of success that by its very definition could not be seen. I once saw her get blood out of a wedding dress when the bride (a neighbour's daughter) had a sudden nosebleed. 'Such a beautiful occasion,' she whispered, rubbing at the glossy satin bodice with her hanky, soothing the girl in the face of her body's criminal failure. Hadn't thought about that for forty years.

I took a roll of film as Lily pulled silly faces in the brilliant birthday sun, so happy, her as well as me. I heard the phone ring; it was early for a Saturday. She had remembered! I was so impressed – but Eleanor's tone was skewed, her words choked, incoherent.

'You're not making any sense.'

She gave me the address of a police station a mile away.

I had been waiting for this moment – not the summons to the police station, because who waits for that, but for a time when there was a fierce clash of interests between my children.

'Is it something bad with Eleanor?' Lily was standing at my side.

'No, darling.'

I would not take Lily to the police station in her birthday dress. She wasn't having that life. I didn't know how best to advise myself. I telephoned Jean. Please don't let her be cross.

'Everything's gone a bit precarious.'

'Oh?'

'Eleanor's been arrested and she wants me to come to the police station.'

'And you've got the party at eleven. Fuck! Let me think for a minute.'

'A minute? I haven't got anything like that long.'

'Tell you what, you go to the station and I'll come over to yours and do the party. Actually, I've got a better idea. You stay with Lily and I'll go to Eleanor. See what they say, see what needs doing.'

'Really? Are you sure?' I thought I might do something unforgivable like cry. Jean *hated* people crying. More than life itself. I started to laugh sombrely.

Later on, while my head was in the fridge coaxing mandarin jellies in their waxed paper cases to set, Jean phoned. I was afraid there might be admonishments, but no.

'Good news. They let her go.'

'Did they? How did she seem?'

'They let her go before I got there. She must have persuaded them.'

'What did they say? What was she meant to have done?'

'They wouldn't tell me much. They were nice, though. Polite.'

'Oh. OK. Good.'

'I'll go through the details with you tomorrow,' Jean said. 'All right? I'm sure your hands are full. It's all quite straightforward.'

Keepings things from people had a bad reputation, but I was grateful.

The following day, the party in bin bags, I rang her back.

'Jean, tell me the truth.'

Eleanor got six months and served just under four. I visited twice and then she asked me not to come again. It was bad there, but I shut down on myself, went on to some kind of automatic setting. My mother had told me her mother told her that Victorian housemaids sometimes woke at seven to find they had already been cleaning out grates and laying fires since ten to five. Perhaps I was like that. I avoided people. It wasn't speakable. I did all right as long as nobody asked how I was. The three people at school who knew were very careful. Mr Machin – geography – made me coffee every morning in a rose-strewn cup and saucer. There weren't really rules for something like this. Jean was quieter with me, controlled, solemn, like a little well-read platinum-haired Buddha. It was time that must be got through, that was all I had to achieve, nothing else whatsoever, she said, apart from keeping my hair on.

At night I couldn't sleep. I avoided my bed with Lily curled up in it. I didn't want her party to the things going through my mind. I felt contagious. I dozed a little in the armchair with a blanket wrapped around me and my own warped panic, waking to the telephone's shrill ring in the hall, diving at it, but there was never anybody at the end of the line. I knew detoxing in prison was considered by some to be an infringement of human rights, but I also knew it was a chance for us. It would be very frightening for Eleanor. She wasn't strong at the best of times. I phoned up now and then although I knew I wasn't allowed, begged to speak to medical staff, just to see how she was doing. The nice receptionist eventually grew stubborn.

'It's not boarding school, love.'

'How would you feel if you were me?'

Jean asked us over every Sunday, although we weren't always up to it. Her heating was cranked up so high it tightened the skin round my eyes. She tried to adopt for us a mildness of manner, flattening herself, agreeing with everything, a steady stream of hot drink requests taken and fulfilled; biscuits, sweeties, felt pens, lip salve. She had those trays they sell in department stores with cushions attached to their undersides. She sat us down in front of bright films with song-and-dance routines, tap steps like gunfire, an assortment of amazing snacks on our laps. 'Just a few odds and ends,' she said. I felt as though I was in a retirement home on an aeroplane. Lily adored it. Sometimes Jean read to us: Babar and Chekhov short stories that seeped into one.

I dreamed I dragged my mattress up to the prison, smoothed down my sheets. Set up camp outside, built a small fire. I just wanted to be where she was. She was the only thing I'd ever had that was all mine. I did wander up there sometimes; it was only fifteen minutes from where we lived. I got as close as I could and stood gazing up at the red brick and the slits of windows, just communing with her, imagining her going about her day, jaunty sometimes, in the bustling kitchens with stainless-steel workstations, wielding a ladle or wiping down greasy tabletops with a dramatic sweep of her cloth, hair pinned back. Or stretched out on her narrow top bunk, eyes buried in a soap; or I saw her racked and shaking with sickness and nausea, bird-like limbs thrashing, night sweats, brutalising headaches and pain in the belly, hair splayed on the pillow like snakes, and I kept rooting for her strenuously – a demented cheerleader, you could say.

The second visit, she held my hand. She had filled out a bit. She had these little cheeks. Sunlight ran over our table and onto the floor of the visitors' centre. I could sit here like this for the rest of my life, I thought. There wasn't much to say. You could see the impact of her good looks on everybody there, that they earned her respect. That they earned me respect also because I was to do with her. I felt proud. I brought a deck of playing cards, but they didn't make it through security. I wished I could hold her properly.

After a while, fearful of creating an atmosphere too laden with silence, I started chatting about any old nonsense: how the man in the corner shop was trying to grow a beard and it just wasn't happening for him; a sudden craze for pastel-coloured pencils smelling like cocktails that had swept the school – piña colada, strawberry daiquiri; my uncertain feelings about Jean's new sheepskin jacket. 'Do I look like a used-car salesman or do I look like a used-car salesman?' she said gleefully. Jean had a new friend I wasn't sure about and she talked about her all the time. Caroline something, double-barrelled. Distant descendant of the Sackville-Wests. 'She's woken some creative hankerings in me,' Jean told me, whatever *that* meant, so I told Eleanor. 'Oh oh! I think she might feel a book coming on.' We giggled together then.

I fed her snippets of news about Lily. I told her how beautifully she had arranged a TV snack recently, as though she were setting up a still life – the fanned pear slices on a glazed green plate, two isosceles triangles of cheese, the cucumber dice, the cluster of black grapes. I told her how she liked to organise clean laundry, the way she folded her blue and pink pants into neat thirds, legs tucked in, the ribbon bows in the centre facing forward always as she stacked the oblongs upright in her chest of drawers. I never heard of a child who did that. I tried to communicate some of the everyday details of her, her lovely ways of doing things, my tone light and silly, until I realised I had made her cry. It might have been me who was crying, I couldn't tell. 'You're doing so well, love,'

I told her, and she looked up and smiled strongly. I could feel the heat of it in my eyes.

'I used to go to the laundrette for you on Sunday afternoons when I was little, didn't I?'

'Yes! Yes, you did! Every week pretty much. It was a lifesaver. I was so grateful.'

'Time's up,' the gruff guard shouted at us.

She let my hand drop abruptly. 'I'll just see you on the out now, Mum. OK?'

I nodded rapidly.

Why did he have to shout?

Lily and I started going for long walks. I couldn't bear to sit waiting in the flat. We wandered into the West End, gazing up at its pale stone splendour, sharing a scoop of lemon sorbet in Piccadilly with our saved bus fares; or we tried to discover a new part of London that we didn't know. We talked as we walked, pointing out strange things, keeping our ears open for funny overhearings and writing them down. 'You've changed your tune!' a woman shouted at her little dachshund. We always took a bag for funny-shaped leaves or impressive conkers; discarded shopping lists Lily especially liked, picking them up from the pavement, poring over them studiously as though they were a guide to life: 1 x coffee, bottle gin, 2 packs streaky bacon (unsmoked), 100 Embassy Mild – that was the best recipe we ever found.

Sometimes she brought the camera Christine had given her for Christmas, a Kodak with an attachable flash, Woolworths' best. It hung round her neck on a thin brown strap, intrepid, professional-looking. She liked to sketch street furniture – decorative drain covers, fire hydrants, railings. She was crazy for gargoyles. We collected shop signs where the sentence order was altered so that the word in the middle came first, like *High-Class Hardware JOHNSON'S and Electrics*. They were feeble outings really, but soothing, steering us through dark clumps of time. One Saturday we walked for a couple of miles east, stopping in front of a large, derelict Victorian house, dark-bricked and double-fronted, symmetrical, a child's drawing of a house but with all its windows plasterboarded and two horizontal sheets of corrugated iron across the front door, like a taped-up mouth. Lily took out her sketchbook and began to draw. It felt very much like the beginning of a story.

'I can see a family of three small girls on the top floor,' I said to her, 'maybe six, eight and ten, in white dresses and the older one very grown up cooking all the dinners in an apron and washing the clothes and setting up a school in the attic with little green benches and slates. In my imagination,' I added.

She nodded reasonably.

The front yard had become a tip for locals; there were two old sinks and a toilet and a broken pram and a small defunct fridge, its door hanging open and inside someone had put an empty tin of cherry Coke. It made a bizarre little outdoor room in the sunshine, weeds and thistles poking through the white enamel. Lily gave the rejected sanitary ware a lot of personality in her drawing, the dulled taps like curious eyebrows, the small plugs mouths, the lavatory the beloved child of the basins possibly, the old house behind them their stage. To the right of the house there was a narrow grassy path, the brick warped and powdery, the grass dotted with pink and white daisies, and we skipped down it like Dorothy and the Scarecrow, pushing open the flaking painted door at the other end, and there – as if by magic – was a long walled garden filled with wild flowers. We peered through the filthy windows into the back of the house. There had clearly been no one living there for some time – just a few sticks of furniture: a rag rug, a green velvet chair, a wooden clothes drier and a marbled enamel bucket in the centre of the room, to catch drips I guessed. Attached to the back of the house was a faded blue-and-white-striped awning with a scalloped edge like you might get outside a cake shop or a park café.

A ragged lawn stretched out, scattered with buttercups and silvery dandelion clocks, and at the end two enormous lilac bushes were in bloom, almost in rivalry. We ran to them and filled our arms with white and purple branches, the flower heads springy and sharp-smelling, fluttering fresh green heart-shaped leaves. Music poured from a radio in a neighbouring garden. A sleepy tortoiseshell cat watched us with disapproving eyes. We rushed home with our stolen treasure, Lily shouldering her burden gamely, not complaining once about the length of the return walk although her arms must have been about to fall off. Mine were. There was such an atmosphere of triumph.

'What would it cost in a shop?' she wanted to know.

'I'm not sure. A lot. Maybe, I don't know, fifty or a hundred quid?'

Her pride in our stolen cargo was immense. She danced round the room, electric with success. She had always delighted in her hunter-gatherer side. At the flat the lilac filled eight jugs, vases and bottles, the tall stems stiff and unbending, spread out like fans, the scent so sweet and heavy and sharp I opened the window to let some of it out. 'Look at it all,' I kept on saying. It was like a brightly painted backdrop to a ballet or, or a beautiful dress shop in an old Hollywood film. We ate some cream cheese and cucumber sandwiches sitting on the front steps, hungry after our exertions. So refreshing! A robin appeared, a Disney robin, hopping over for the crumbs. I put a little apricot jam in a teacup and gave it to Lily with a spoon.

When we went back in, the scent hit me powerfully. It wasn't a million miles from moth repellent, I conceded, eyes watering, nose tingling, sharpness at the back of my throat. I had put the dark and the light flowers together, but the contrast suddenly looked too harsh, like a football strip or something, a crass flag, and I worked out it looked better with the colours separate. None of the lilac was actually lilac – that very pale and delicate silvery mauve-pink I loved – but bright white and a slightly sinister deep Vatican purple. That suddenly upset me, felt like the end of the world. How could I mind something so silly? And then I minded that I minded so much more than I cared about the colour of the flowers. And then I wanted it all to be more fragile and frothy; these heads were hulking, dense and snout-like. Rings of disappointment bled out of me.

'Don't worry, don't worry,' Lily said, kissing my cheek. 'Not at all bad for free, remember!'

Later on, when I tried to jiggle the stems around to try to make the whole thing look looser and more natural, I realised the branches were alive with tiny crawling bugs. It was the last straw. I fought back more tears. Still, 'A hundred pounds,' Lily murmured now and then, marvelling, half outraged, as though we had somehow been overcharged. 'Just can't BELIEVE it.'

That cheered me and I started to debug the branches. Oddly familiar work, a bit like picking nits out of girl hair. 'Let me help you.' Lily rolled up her sleeves.

*

I read that coming out of prison was the most dangerous time of all because your tolerance went right down while you were inside. I went to meet Eleanor on the morning she was released, clutching a small bunch of wild flowers, a food parcel, a novel Jean recommended, but she had gone. Amazing that capacity she had to make you feel like a mad hanger-on, even at the prison gates. That you were intruding. The female guard smirked. Oh look, another sad fuck.

I telephoned her every other day for two weeks; she didn't once answer. It was almost as though *my* tolerance was depleted. I was in a dangerous state, not sleeping, not eating. I went to her doorstep quite often in my lunch hour – left things there for her, fruit, once a cake in a white box, a loaf and some cheese wrapped in a cloth, milk, eggs. Or I just sat there and hummed quietly to myself, a fantasy of intimacy, a hymn or an old folk song to keep me going. I sometimes saw her standing by the top-floor window, which was reassuring. I didn't need much.

I wrote her a letter, pouring out my hopes and fears. I talked about the time she was born. I spoke of her father's lack of interest in me, of my own father's, which made me for a time unwell. That I wasn't proud of the way I had handled that side of things. Our fatherlessness an hereditary disease.

I referred to other mistakes I had made: my capacity for false intuition and the more unfortunate aspects of my character, the way I sometimes found it hard to accept myself. I fell on my sword from as many angles as I could, that I was sorry I wasn't of a finer grain. How I shouldn't have needed so much from her when she was small, that it had not been fair on my part, weighing her down with responsibility. That I had made her live in that terrible street, which had been blind of me. I allowed myself one line of reproach and it was this: *You won't risk yourself, and because of that you live in a state of permanent risk. We all do.* I put forward a plan for our lives, the three of us, all that they might be, seeing as there was so much potential. I spoke of treatment, a new life in the country as a proper family, by the seaside, in a different town, another continent. *Whatever you want I will do. Whatever it takes. However mad it may sound, I need your help now. PLEASE. I cannot keep going as we are. Love Mum.*

I popped out to the postbox on the corner with the letter, fed it through the narrow slit, walked back home bone-weary, bone-forlorn. Straight away a curdling anxiety, botched intentions, grave errors churning, elements of distrust and dismay. Was I threatening her? I couldn't tell. Why couldn't I? There are no lies that wound as deeply as the lies we tell ourselves. Or was that not true? I couldn't think straight. I couldn't sit, I couldn't sleep. Cowering, I watched the clock mark each minute from eleven until five, when I rose and read a book, I couldn't say what it was, poring over the arrangement of neat black marks on the page until they started to resemble little bugs. I had never made a distinction between books and life before, I always thought it was the same, but now I wasn't sure. How had I not realised reading was a way of shutting your eyes to reality, of shrinking things and hiding?

At ten to seven I slipped on some plimsolls and walked out of the flat with my raincoat over my nightdress. It was cool and silent on the street, a starkness to the early light, and I waited for the postman to make his first collection. His old van rattled into view eventually. He was spry and lanky with a long, bounding stride. He had a cap, he had an actual sack and I begged him to let me have the letter.

'Oh yes?' he said, opening up the cage inside the postbox with ominous keys.

'It's my daughter. Can't put a foot right. You know what it's like. They're sent to try us, I suppose.'

His expression remained impassive. You'll have to do better than that.

'Thought I would explain things in a letter, put my side, but sleeping on it I'm pretty sure it will only make everything worse. I may have come on a bit strong. Might do her head in. Things have been tricky for a while, you could say. It will pass. Hardly unusual. But I think the letter may have been a mistake.'

He was staring at me, hard to read. The sky was beginning to wake up slowly, a grey and white streaked haze thickening. 'I'm not the best mum in the world.' It was such a relief to confess it finally! My voice sounded elated.

I could tell that the less needy I appeared, the more he would be inclined to give. (Welcome to the human race.) 'I mean, see what you think, of course,' I murmured. 'Probably just me being silly.' Then, pointing lightly: 'It's that blue envelope there.'

He drew the moment out: he could not resist. I stood red-cheeked, my bare legs bluish in the morning chill, until he smiled handsomely and said, 'Oh go on then, Mum.' I liked that he called me Mum. Bet he had a lovely one at home, making giant cooked breakfasts so he didn't outgrow his strength. I hoped he did. There was something a bit noble about him. He handed the letter back and I thanked him, but then he shook his head at me and I felt the sting all through my body. I stumbled slightly. I began to shake my head at me too. He walked away, light-footed, light-hearted as he opened the door of his bright van to escape me, and then he paused and turned round. 'Be lucky!' he called out. That made me really smile. He didn't have to do that.

That summer it rained funerals. 'They're not as bad as weddings,' Jean said. 'At least the damage is already done.'

Luke went first, Christine's husband. It was that awful thing when someone doesn't appear to be very ill and it's the treatment that kills them. He was so shrunken at the very end it was hard not to think of films I'd seen at school of the camps. He was sixty-six. I'd heard from Sarah he was going downhill and I rang the bell of the house one afternoon and Christine asked if I would like to sit with him. Just like that. There wasn't anything left to say, but I perched at the end of the bed and rubbed his feet for half an hour or so as the room grew dark and shadowy. I felt as though I were in a dream; sitting on the edge of their world, Christine's cold cup of coffee on the bedside table, her thin lawn nightdress, a tube of ointment for cracked heels, several bottles of pills, an apple on a yellow saucer with a knife. Cards and letters from friends and neighbours to say goodbye were scattered on the bedspread. A splayed Conrad novel on the floor looked warm, as though she had been reading it to him before I arrived. The remnants of her frugal lunch. I had often imagined their life together and it was incredible to find myself installed among their scenery and props.

I tried to warm his icy feet in my hands. They were ash-coloured, pale and charcoal ashes mixed, and the skin seemed to darken with my touch. I tucked his feet back into the sheet and the blanket and the coverlet, putting them to bed like twins. I picked up the chair and moved it soundlessly next to the pillow. I leaned forward and stroked his hair. I felt like a thief, but he seemed easy. Did he know someone was there? Did he know it was me? I scarcely knew myself but I could tell it was close to the end. Another frozen half-hour passed. I allowed myself to think he might have decided to give me something, finally. There was a saving pure beauty to the scene I thought, and then I killed the thought because it wasn't true. It was so hard in life to know what to allow yourself, but it had the feeling of a sacrament.

Being with someone who was close to dying was oddly akin to waiting to give birth. That same concentration and the effort involved and the slowing of reality and the open texture of everything. Trying to rise to the vastness of the occasion and the sense that the stakes were too high for me or that I was too young for such levels of responsibility, that anyone would be. So much responsibility not letting him go. Much of my life had been spent keeping people alive, I realised.

I could scarcely believe that I who had been so roundly fenced away was being given such intimate privileges now. But Christine needed a break from her vigil; perhaps that was all it was. I could hear her light footsteps on the floor above. I was a great one for allocating meaning where there was none. She had been sitting there for sixteen hours, it transpired, was delighted when she saw me. I could have been anyone.

An exchange in Christine's car: we were eighteen, it was summer and we were on our way to her grandmother's birthday. There were to be eighty guests and lunch in a tent with pink tables on the lawn. Christine had dressed me up in her clothes. It was a beautiful day but I felt anxious and uncertain. Her family had those brittle English manners that always seemed to me more like bullying. 'I will be able to sit next to you, won't I?' I asked nervously. We slowed into a long queue of traffic and she looked at me with utter fury. '*I can't promise you that!*' I had often felt her voice sharpen itself against me.

I shut down my thoughts and gave myself over to dream-like communion. Streams of confused memories moving through the room, stolen things emerging, shapeless, half-remembered ghost emotions. A sense I was experiencing new things I had lived before, that there was no difference between the past and the present, or rather the differences seemed smaller than the similarities, but then what was I actually losing? So hard to know when you didn't understand what it was, who it was you had missed. And then death and Eleanor to me were so fully entwined that once or twice I almost believed it was her body lying next to me. That was what I had readied myself for. 'Sweetheart,' I called out to her, but of course she wasn't there. That was an enormous blessing.

Then I heard the death rattle, as clearly as I had heard my mother's with the baby clamped tightly to my chest more than thirty years ago, and I began to count the seconds between the breaths. It was going to happen. I stood and called to Christine to come down.

'I'll sit in the kitchen,' I murmured, my voice hoarse, just a thread. I wasn't sure I could control myself. I had spent decades safeguarding his privacy and to squander it now? I smoothed a crease in the thick white French bed cover, adjusting the spare pillow gently so it sat square next to his head. I wanted to do everything properly. 'I'll make you some tea.'

'No,' she said. 'Please stay.' I knew I did not have the right to be in the room when he died – to be part of the facts of his death. To have a share in them. That was too great a trespass against how we had all lived, but I had to do as she asked. I thought it was right. I hoped it was, but I was trembling.

As he lay cooling, she moved the chair back to the foot of the bed and began to sketch him with charcoal. The sound of the drawing was rapid and breathy, like the sound of a small animal hiding its food. I did leave the room then. I went downstairs and opened the French windows at the back of the kitchen, wandered into the garden. A few early blackberries were out and the birds were making the most of them. I picked some sprigs of rosemary with tiny pale blue flowers, for remembrance, holding my fingers up to my nose. I filled the kettle and put it on the gas. The flame was the same colour as their delphiniums.

His boys carried him at the end with great dignity. They were so like him, how he used to be when he was young, that at first I couldn't look and then I couldn't stop looking. They were tall and serious now. He always said he was waiting for them to deepen themselves, even when they were seven and five. The eldest, Ruben, was with his heavily pregnant girlfriend and her mother. First time either of them had worn suits, Christine said.

I sat with Christine after the wake, feeding her sips of brandy in the kitchen, with Fran and Sarah in grey and navy, as though they'd never quite moved on from our school uniform. They weren't as good with her as I was, I thought, their gestures amateurish and clumsy. They didn't realise that although you had to soften yourself with someone in shock, you also needed to be clear and predictable, all your actions smooth and certain like neat teacher's print. They mumbled, which meant things had to be repeated three or four times. They kept standing up and sitting down, offering Christine things she didn't want, asking her questions that didn't mean anything. There couldn't be anything sudden at a moment like this. I tried to seem more like a light breeze than a person, a woman. Christine was stunned, almost catatonic at first, and all I could do was make sure she was warm. I put on some cello music, played it quietly like reading a story in the background, wrapped her in a shawl, draped my cardigan over her shoulders as her skin was like ice, laid a blanket on her lap. She held my hand tightly.

'Should we go?' Sarah mouthed to me, Fran mouthed. There was a sense that I was a professional in this realm.

'It's up to you. I feel confident. Whatever you think . . . I'm easy.'

They gathered their things.

Later on she began to talk wildly, her hands making violent jagged movements, as though they had been stung or burned, or she was trying to reach or strike something out of her grasp. They seemed despairing. It was painful to observe. She was troubled in particular by the years they had spent apart, decades ago now. 'What if that was the best time in his life?' she cried. 'The time away?' It was out of character for her to think anything against herself, let alone say it, but I knew all the ways grief assaulted the personality. I couldn't answer. I had spent a bit of time with him myself during that period. He liked my company for a while and then he really didn't.

I knew better than to say *Of course those years weren't the best, I'm sure he was miserable without you and the boys, you're out of your mind. Or why did he come back? And you have to remember you're in shock and when you've just had the rug pulled out from under, your thoughts and feelings, well, they just aren't reliable!* I knew she needed someone to hear her painful thoughts, to allow the difficult things to stand without anyone batting them away. At least I thought she did, but when I did not contradict her, she began to wail. It was vague and unspecific, the sort of crude anger and recriminations I associated with loss, but it was not the first time in my life I wasn't certain what she knew. I stood and took it, bowing my head, apologising for the way she was feeling, reassuring, softly and widely, without naming anything. It was a relief in its way. Then suddenly she turned mischievous and rueful. 'At least I'll be able to put the lights on now. That is something. We used to have these dreadful rows.'

'How do you mean?'

'"Why do you always leave the lights on?" I don't *leave* them on, I *put* them on. You know. There's a difference. How trivialising to have to have that conversation as a grown woman. Lights make the house seem warm and welcoming, like a home almost. Ideally I would get this sensation from the building's other inhabitants, but until I do I like to fall back on electricity.'

'SO good!' I said, and she seized my hands in friendship and we laughed madly and the moment passed. I fed her more sips of Luke's brandy and we had Brazil nuts and chunks of cheese and chocolate raisins to soak it up. Everything tasted so delicious. I held my glass up to the light and heard myself propose a toast to his health, and the minute I said it I realised what I had done. Christine did get angry with me then, and she roared, 'For Christ's sake, Ruth, you need to think before you open your fucking mouth!' For mouth I half heard legs.

The tempo of the evening altered abruptly. I started shaking. My drink went over and the glass cracked into three. The seconds stretched out and I feared some other kind of breakage. I thought she might strike me and I began to apologise wildly on and on, for anything and everything, picking up the pieces of glass and wrapping them carefully in newsprint, and gradually her evil look melted into a frown and then the frown lines softened into a half-smile, and before long we laughed and laughed and laughed, it was all so mad and dangerous.

I made him spaghetti with clams once. It was the day after his birthday and I was wearing my good dress. The clams were expensive and I rinsed them about fifty times in cold water to get rid of every last piece of grit. I steamed them in white wine with a small amount of garlic and olive oil and bright dots of chilli and watched the shells relax themselves and open in the warmth. I felt hopeful. I mixed in the three-quarters-cooked spaghetti and muddled it all together, threw in two handfuls of chopped flat-leaf parsley, twists of black pepper, the shells clanking crisply in the pan, I ladled it into blue and white soup plates, bent the pan forward to scoop up the juices, leaning away to avoid the steam, but instead of a light milky colour at the bottom, the liquid was dark grey, almost black. I couldn't risk it. I stood over the pedal bin, scraping out the bowls. A broad ladder sprinted up my new tights, my leg pale and failing bluish through the rungs. I made him egg on toast instead. I remember he swore.

After I left Christine's, I went straight over to Eleanor's. I wanted to pour myself out to her, but as I turned into her street I changed my mind. I mustn't be selfish; she wasn't strong. I couldn't have it both ways. She didn't need anything else difficult in her life. I longed for flares of intimacy and kinship but she wasn't that kind of daughter. She was shadowy and powerful; like any ghost worth its salt, she made you feel that *you* were the intruder. Since she had come out of prison there were even more locks and bars on her. Besides, we never talked to each other about death. It was too strong a current in our life to be named.

Then a girl at school. To see not just someone's parents and siblings but her grandmother and great-grandmother at the funeral, clinging to each other, twins in their ivory crêpe blouses and old-fashioned black jackets with stiff shoulders, veins of despair throbbing violet on the backs of their hands, marks of woe on their faces. I had never seen anything like it. The older lady, ancient and stooping, face like flour beneath a pillbox hat, trembling wan costumed outrage – that nature could have permitted it. Thin white wisps of hair. It was an insult beyond her comprehension. I wondered if she felt it made a mockery of all she had endured in her life. I would feel that, I think. Her daughter, the grandmother, visibly religious, passing beads noiselessly back and forth between her palms. Poppy, the girl in question, not quite fourteen. She had suffered some sort of one-in-a-million heart event in the middle of the night. Perfectly healthy. A lovely girl, warm, bright-hearted.

I spoke to the parents at the funeral and they were from a different planet to the older pair: singing her praises fluently, sobbing in between sentences with no self-censure, smiling and wiping their noses on their sleeves, expressions of gratitude bright in the air where you might have expected bitter curses. To have the sort of loss that allowed you to be loving outwardly, to seize another's hands, holding on to everything offered so strongly, almost as though teaching a new dance, gathering everybody in, without shame, to be that generous in receiving consolation, completely open-hearted, during the throes of tragedy. It was beyond imagining. Loss did not make this couple desolate and punishing. They were comradely. I was so inspired. I just nodded and nodded and my eyes were wet too and I told them how lovely and amazing she was at school, brightening, cheering, soaring. Poppy's tiny sisters chased round the garden, for now, oblivious.

Another amazing thing – they had decorated the coffin with photographs of her, like a scrapbook or collage, and there were baby pictures, then a toddler feeding a tangle of noodles to a chicken on her auntie's farm, birthday cakes aflame, snaps of her as a snail with rolled grey stripy duvet shell in *The Insect Play*, a clipping from the local paper when she had done her cycling proficiency and had been photographed with fourteen other children and the shy lady mayor swamped by civic chains. The wonderful thing was that after the service everyone assembled round the coffin, making slow circuits of it, pointing things out to each other with delight. They had Xeroxed a prize-winning project she had done at school on the paintings of Queen Elizabeth I. There she was with a department store Santa, sullen in his muddy brown trainers while she grinned. She was caught in a handstand in her marigold leotard with the three BAGA badges sewn down one side. In cross-hatched shadows of the Eiffel Tower she stood squinting into the overdeveloped sunshine. She was all of her there. People were usually terrified of coffins and it was extraordinary to have drawn everybody close to her body at this moment, celebrating her exactly where she was lying at the last. A table piled with ladylike cakes went completely ignored. Poppy she was called. Poppy Richardson.

That coffin killed death a little bit.

SEVEN

It was mid November, another year over, Christmas was ticking, Lily and I were clinging on. Jean had grown closer to her new friend Caroline something double-barrelled; a poet and agitator was how she liked to be styled. Jean was all *Caroline says, Caroline thinks*. They went on fancy outings together: private views, opening nights. One Sunday they drove to Charleston, Caroline in stunning colours, *fearlessly* attired. The pink of the dining table impressed Jean with its *fierce whimsy*, the winter borders she pronounced *divine*. (What had happened to my old friend who thought gardening outdoor housework?) When Jean said, 'Caroline likes a velvet cigarette pant in the evening,' I thought, this won't end well.

Jean had taken to wearing long floaty scarves, not unusual in the more mature woman, certainly, but these ones were verging on the Guineverian, just over her old sheepskin coat. Caroline seemed to have an endless supply, like an end-of-the-pier magician. Jean looked – well, she looked mad. She looked *well* mad, in fact, but she was happy. She had those glowing brick-pink circles in her cheeks Lily had when she was teething. She was trying a new apple-flavour two-in-one conditioning shampoo, she told me. A dab of violet scent did I detect? I started to wonder if it was a love affair she was having. Once or twice – unheard of, this – she had been late for school. She had a sort of hazy, questioning vagueness to her now. There was that sense of a phone call from abroad with a delay. She asked you the same thing two or three times. 'Could you see me in a chandelier earring?' Her form was merciless.

'Ruth, my angel, I do believe you're jealous,' Mr Machin – geography – said at school, brushing biscuit crumbs from his autumn-coloured cords.

'Could you be a little jealous?' Christine said, Sarah said, and Fran, when we met for a slightly dismal drink, ostensibly to Cheer Christine Up.

'Jealous?' I boomed. 'Of that utterly ridiculous person?' I sighed audibly. 'Please don't make me laugh.' My derision fell flat though because my nonchalant hand gesture knocked over and shattered a whole bottle of white wine. They knew it was serious then. A tiny waitress sank to her knees with cloth, mop and dustpan, apologising.

I thought about Caroline sometimes when I was falling asleep, trying to tease out inconsistencies. She was a low-level irritant, a gnat with inflated ideas about itself, a football team I would not wear the scarf of even if caught in a freak blizzard. The facts of her scraped against my nerves. She detested Wordsworth yet she was a terrific fan of psychoanalysis? That didn't work. She did not believe in umbrellas – they were a suburban invention; well, she could take it from me that they existed. She thought women with a sweet tooth trivialised themselves. What, all of them? (Jean would have to curb her cake habit – why should she?) She objected to English people who hadn't grown up in London. She despised the word 'very' because it de-intensified and people didn't realise. Couldn't *countenance* pelmets. She liked scuffed brogues, left-overs, pinstripes, neat whisky, old Soho, the squeak of tulip stalks, tomato sandwiches for every meal (she'd stolen that straight out of F. Scott Fitzgerald). She said a femme fatale should have a laugh that was alluring and dismissive. She loved all swear words except 'Christ!' – which was blasphemous. There were biographies of most of her relations, lined up on a shelf in the lav, Jean said, which had beautiful eighteenth-century toile de Jouy material gathered in a little skirt round the sink. Sounded awfully dingy to me.

The stories were already wearing thin, shop-soiled. Caroline's great-grandmother said to her grandmother, 'Darling, you do not have to marry money, but you must marry where money *is*.' So odd that Caroline would want such idiocy known. She was a cross between Nancy Mitford and Enoch Powell. Odd to be an expert on someone's catalogue of likes and dislikes without even having met the person. I bet she hadn't studied poetry, spent years at the coal face writing three practical criticisms a week as I had done, taking every line ending, every stray comma to task in echoey rooms in Gower Street. I used to race back to my mum's after college via the market, where there were always rich pickings around half four when they were packing up. I'd make food, chat with her a minute, settle her down, get changed, head off to my job at the restaurant. It was a good life! Had Caroline a Masters in colour words in Anglo-Saxon poetry from Oxford like Jean? I sincerely doubted it. I hoped with all my heart her poems were no good. Wasn't I evil?

Jean invited me to a recital Caroline was giving in a little café bar in Earls Court, but I had a parents' evening at Lily's school that night. Small mercies. If she was going to try out being a lesbian, why had she chosen someone so far-fetched? What was wrong with the nice woman in the health food shop? I was meticulously polite to Jean, of course I was. I always enquired as to Caroline's health, for example, when we spoke, or the specific poetic forms she favoured currently (November was villanelle month – *hooray*), her preferred methods of agitation and so on, even if the very mention of her name made me want to vomit.

Jean lost a lot of weight.

'I feel lighter about life generally. It feels more. *I* feel more. Try to be pleased for me.'

'Of course,' I said, 'it's amazing,' but my true feelings betrayed me on the second syllable, a snigger reared its ugly head and I somehow pronounced the word 'amarzing', which sounded as though I was taking the piss. Oh dear. I faked a small coughing fit to help us both over the moment.

When would Jean see through her?

Suddenly Jean started walking everywhere. Three miles to work, three miles all the way home. At weekends she got the bus to Primrose Hill and tramped up to the top then down into Regent's Park then across into Hyde Park, then Green Park then St James's. 'Buckingham Palace is so ugly,' she said. 'Poor old Queen.' She bought a cashmere coat to ward off the cold; it was of such high quality the wool had a sleek, shimmering appearance. What would she do if it rained? Two sets of fine knitted silk thermals she ordered from a catalogue. A corduroy hand warmer, like a small hot-water bottle you heated in the microwave. She bought a microwave.

'So sportive, Jean!' I said.

'Don't mock me.'

One night she telephoned. It was late. I was alarmed. Lily

sprang out of bed and I ushered her back into the bedroom with the cable wrapped around me. My hand over the receiver, I tucked her back in, smoothed her down. 'It's just Jean ringing for a chat. Nothing to worry.' I kissed her, closed the door.

'You will be pleased to hear,' Jean spoke theatrically, 'Caroline and I are no longer friends.'

'No, Jean, no! God. I am so sorry.'

'No you're not.'

'Well, I'm not proud of that.'

'And you know she was about ten times more dishonest than any man I've ever met.'

'Was she? The villain!'

'Yes, she was rather.'

'Well, they do say poets are worse even than painters.'

'Do they?'

'Oh yes.'

'You just made that up!' Jean's sad laughter was so endearing.

'Sorry I've been a bit . . . terrible of late.'

'Yes. Yes you have,' she said. 'But I forgive you.'

'Thanks. That is very handsome.'

I had a powerful feeling suddenly that I wanted to buy her an enormous present. Something really astounding like, I don't know, a huge ruby or a Picasso or a lion.

Jean's capacity to bounce back in life always impressed me. The way she held herself in high regard. It was a form of personal, almost bodily optimism, you could say. Integrity that went deep and was to be admired. She knew herself well, of course, not just her likes and dislikes but the way her various wounds quickened things in her that might not help a situation. She put all her self-knowledge to good use. She had been kind to her weaknesses in life, and perhaps because of that they scarcely troubled her any more. They had come up in the world.

'How's herself anyway?' she asked.

'Haven't seen her for so long. Must be almost sixteen months. I just have to try not to—'

'I meant the little one.'

'She's . . . well, she's reasonable.'

That autumn term as she moved into Year 4, Lily's handwriting went from a beautifully deliberate cursive script to something ill-aligned and spidery. 'She's got the writing of a gin-and-cigarettes novelist who's haunted by past love affairs and given away her son,' Jean said.

'Oh!'

'Sorry sorry sorry,' she said. 'Fuck fuck fuck. I don't know *where* that came from. I think it's the most tactless thing I ever heard.'

'It's up there, Jean.'

I decided to get Eleanor for Christmas. Surely she could watch TV on the sofa in a blanket with Lily on her lap for three quarters of an hour, unwrap a few Quality Street, pull a cracker, suffer the indignity of the paper hat? We could all doze in front of *The Wizard of Oz*, swathed in wrapping and ribbon, prising royal icing off slabs of crumbling fruit cake, imitate the scarecrow's lazy grace. Even a grave invalid, in an emergency, could make the bed-hangers sense there was a bit more to the story, for a short span of time; they could rally, forge smiles and feeble jokes to soften things for others, if the desire was there. Show love. That was all it would take. Lily's mother had something I could not give her.

'Are you sure?' Jean said. 'Why don't you both come to Louisa's with me? You'd be doing me a favour. You know she rations my potatoes, but she wouldn't dare if you were there. Once she actually took some off my plate with her fork. You could stick up for me – "That's the perfect amount of potatoes, actually. It's what they recommended on Radio 4." She'd listen to you. Her youngest, Izzy, is rather amazing. Funny and clever. Reads all day long.'

'Thanks so much. It's a lovely offer, but I think we'd better keep a bit quiet this year.'

At night Lily and I huddled together, immersed. The softness of her skin, her breath on my cheek, the long, hot limbs, the hair so silky it was like Sindy hair. I lay awake wondering if she would ever dare to be naughty. Should I encourage it? I used to lie awake wondering the same about her mum. Eleanor was very nurturing to me when she was little, looking out for me when I was really struggling, taking the temperature of my days. She was so dutiful. I should have stopped it. I had done the same for my own mother, but I knew it wasn't right. My mother was fearful: the only person I'd ever heard of who unplugged the radio when there was thunder and lightning. She would jump a foot in the air when a door slammed or someone dropped a spoon. She had been bold though in her youth. Her favourite thing when she was little was tying people's feet together under the table with bootlaces and string!

'Do you think Lil looks a bit sad around the eyes?' I asked Jean. 'Please be honest with me.'

'I think she looks like someone who knows life is a serious business, perhaps a few years before she might.'

I swore under my breath.

I drove over to Eleanor's on the 19th of December. No one answered when I rang the bell, but I had my book and I waited half an hour in the car until I saw her walking slowly up the street with another blank girl. They both wore grey clothes head to toe, crumpled military-looking coats with flaps and buckles, an array of cold colours in their skin. I got out of the car, balanced my mug of coffee on the bonnet, waved my arms at the pair.

'Hello there!' I called over to her. Eleanor looked up sharply. The light was so bright I could barely see her eyes.

'MUM!' she cried, and came rushing towards me, and I turned behind me for a brief second, checking it wasn't designed for anyone else, her magnificent greeting, but there was no one about.

I smiled as hard as I could then and we threw our arms round each other. Her skin was icy but her welcome was so hot I thought it might leave marks. I was very grateful. I started kissing her head all over then stopped myself abruptly. I slipped a couple of notes into her jeans. She invited her friend to join in the hug, although I got the sense they barely knew each other. Her friend was something of a stranger to a cake of soap, I thought stingily. Her name appeared to be Hig and/or Higgy or Higs, which was oddly Beatrix Potter-ish.

'So . . . Christmas,' I said, my tone very bright. 'Food around two and we'll collect you at half one while the bird is resting? Lucky beast! That sound OK? I'll ring you in the morning to remind you around eleven if I may. I'm making my famous cranberry and orange sauce.' My nerves made an idiot of me some-times, as though they were invested in everything disintegrating.

Eleanor turned to her friend who had a pronounced uncertain look.

'You'll come, won't you?' she said.

Higs or Higgy nodded.

'Great,' I said a little more weakly. 'See you next Saturday. Don't have a big breakfast, guys!'

Guys?

Christmas morning, Lily opened her stocking and we had saucers of bacon and tangerine segments and chocolate money as Eleanor and I always used to. Lily had made me a board game for Christmas. It was multicoloured, with pistachio, lilac and apricot squares, button counters, two red and gold dice. It was absolutely brilliant. The aim of the game was to go through life notching up glories of the career and family variety. *Have twins. Congratulations!* One of the white bonus cards said, *Take a job as a brain surgeon. Move forward four squares!*

Lunchtime came. I had bought the smallest turkey in the world – a turkinette, we called it – but it was still a turkey, crisp and burnished as it emerged from the oven, and I set it on my mother's oval blue and white flowery plate with the gold rim and turned up the heat for the spuds. We drove to Eleanor's, rang the bell repeatedly, singing a dreadful modern carol Lily had taught me: 'Joseph, Mary, what you gonna do? Joseph, Mary, you'll never find bed and breakfast for two . . . ' We rang the bell and knocked the knocker, our voices getting frailer; we waited outside for ten minutes, but she didn't come. *Move backwards three squares.*

We didn't refer to it between ourselves: pride, tact, fear. When we got home the flat felt overheated from the efforts of the oven, the heat heavy, full of dust, the air downtrodden. Everything looked shabby and awful. Would I ever have the energy to sand the floor? I threw open the window roughly. I allowed myself a moment of anger, but I didn't take myself up on the offer. The potatoes were perfect, twenty-four-carat gold, but neither of us had much in the way of appetite. 'Feel sorry for the turkinette,' Lily said.

'Yeah.'

At seven o'clock, Lily poured herself a glass of water, went into the bedroom, closed the door. The next thing I heard was a scream.

I ran in. 'Lily! What's happened?'

'Nothing,' she said. 'Sorry. Just felt like screaming, so I did.'

At nine o'clock, a rather feeble wail of carols in our street, and I went down and opened the front door to – Jean! I sensed she was on the cusp of some insufferable pun, all wrapped up in her red and green scarf – 'long as you've got your elf', that sort of thing – but she curtailed herself. I wasn't sure I could stomach it just now.

'How was Louisa's?' I asked her as we went up the stairs.

'Not bad. Goose, she served us – a status roast apparently. Never had it before. Izzy made the pudding, which tasted quite sausagey, but a good effort all round. Those boys are evil little capitalists though. Set up a Christmas casino and won all Izzy's presents off her but I made them give everything back. They rather live in fear of my high-court-judge side. You'll be glad to hear.' She smiled. I had the feeling she had actually had a wonderful time and was being tactful.

'Tea, coffee, wine, cyanide?'

'I'm good,' she said. 'How did you get on here?'

'It was . . . ' I sighed. 'Yeah.'

'Christmas comes round very fast, doesn't it?'

I nodded.

Jean had a large white box for Lily and we carried it into the front room, Lily almost hyperventilating. 'Your excitement is very polite!' Jean said. Inside, wrapped in green tissue, was a small orange cast-iron saucepan, a five-inch metal frying pan, a blue and white enamel slotted spoon and six jam jars with red-and-white-checked lids containing : rice, macaroni, raisins, flour (s/r), flour (p), lentils.

Lily grinned. 'Jesus! It's grown-up cookings!'

I nodded, grinning also, but then I pictured her leaving home, with a large suitcase and a limp raincoat, sleeves rolled to the elbow, like a little evacuee. I clutched my ribs. The high emotions of Christmas I could never master.

Still, 'Damn you're good,' I said to Jean.

When Lily was asleep, we chatted softly on the sofa, our sips of wine interspersed with great woolly yawns. 'You going to be all right?' Jean said.

'I expect so.' I nodded. Then, after a few seconds, 'You?'

'I've never quite believed there was an alternative.'

'That's true enough.'

'No word from Alan at all.'

'Oh, I'm sorry to hear that.'

'I was sorry too, but then I remembered an argument we had where he said I only went into teaching so I could get paid for being in the right all the time.'

'God!'

'I mean, he had a point I suppose.'

'Yeah . . . no.'

She looked at me carefully. 'You ever wish that you'd . . .' I waited for more, but her question politely disintegrated. But then, although no more words were forthcoming, she tilted her head slightly and suddenly what she'd asked me picked up its current and expanded wildly.

I smiled a huge smile. 'Of course I do. All the time!'

Jean started laughing then and I laughed too and we shook our heads at ourselves rapidly and the next thing I knew I was waking up under a blanket and it was four o'clock in the morning and there was a little green-ink note from Jean on the rug that said *Happy Boxing Day my brilliant friend*. I felt Christmas fizzing all through my body then as though there was tinsel instead of veins and bells ringing madly and pine needles in my hair. Better late than never. I went into the kitchen, detached a leg from the turkinette and ate it in my fingers over the sink, grease all down my chin, like Henry VIII.

Time wore on; what else could it do? Lily was eleven now, a strong and thoughtful person. Her face very clear, frank and open, smooth, symmetrical, with huge dark-blue-grey intelligent eyes, careless-looking golden hair, dancer's limbs. She moved to my school, which made me happy. An office romance, I thought to myself, until she sat me down one night and asked me, formally, to treat her as I treated everyone else. 'Of course.' No free cuddles in the corridors then. Fine! Her earnestness, because it had a strange heaviness to it, diluted her looks slightly, which was good, I thought. They were in need of diluting. They were pacing themselves. Her vast eyes were so long-lashed people often asked if she wore mascara. Why didn't they comment on the thoughtful look she had, the things she noticed, her excellent conversation: 'Who would you say of all the people you know was most like you in your character, Ruth?' she asked me as we went round the supermarket. 'What would a world look like that had no racism in?' her voice low and earnest in the biscuit aisle. 'Would it even be recognisable?' 'Ruth, would *you* ban nuclear weapons if it was down to you?' I nodded my head. She put her hand on my hand that was steering the trolley. 'I would too,' she said approvingly.

She prided herself on being a good friend, but the lengths she went to, I just wasn't sure. Could you be too loyal in life? 'Her dad bought her a football and she literally hasn't been interested in football for months. What was he thinking?! Well, he wasn't thinking, was he?' She sounded a hundred years old at such moments. Playground disputes she spoke of with compassion better suited to the sorrows of the battlefield.

I telephoned Jean. 'Look, Ruth,' she was reassuring, 'what you have to remember is this is a child whose favourite colour is yellow, a child who repaints her toenails every Sunday afternoon; what's more she is someone who routinely adds an exclamation mark to the end of her name.' It was true her cards and little notes were often signed *Love Lily!* like a 1950s gingham-hearted TV show.

'By the way,' Jean added, 'ought one of us point out they are considered bad style?'

'Shut up, Jean!' I cried.

We had a telephone in the hall by the front door and Lily stood there cradling the red coiled cable, teasing out the strands of tiny slights and disputes until some possibility of justice was glimpsed. She had a fondness for all that was correct. The proper channels: negotiation, mediation, reparation. She was a sort of playground magistrate. It was possible I saw reproaches to me in her great narratives of consolation concerning broken pencil cases and missing netball socks. Her own disappointments we barely spoke of, but we both knew they were of a different scale. Sometimes she left the phone off the hook to buy herself some peace. 'She's just working things out,' Jean said, 'perfectly natural. Trying to make calculations, distinctions and measurements. It's dignified,' she said. 'And it's clever. Your Lily is a young person for whom dignity is very important. She's discriminating. That's a good instinct.' Jean's daughter had a 'Don't sweat the small stuff' fridge magnet that made Jean want to slit her wrists.

Lily had taken to falling asleep to radio phone-in shows at bed-time. There was a different one every night, the host presenting a tender ear to his loyal listeners. She liked the Saturday one, the help's at hand, which concerned itself with answers to low-level domestic disasters: how to get red wine out of pale carpets and upholstery, how to make your ageing grouting gleam – problems to which the solutions were often white wine vinegar and soda crystals. There was a health one with homespun cures for arthritis and gout. I sensed she was equipping herself for life.

Christine's parents' house had a large sloping attic. We went up there once in the middle of the night, a bit drunk. We found a torch and when I shone it round I was amazed to see everything she might ever need when she grew up: flowery armchairs with home-made cushions, a rocking horse, bookcases filled with children's books, an old sewing machine, paintings not considered good enough for downstairs but still impressive, a lemon-yellow Formica kitchen table . . . It was like her own personal department store. I shut my eyes for a minute, in jealousy I suppose it was, and there was something more pointed also, a distaste that she seemed to feel entitled to it all.

I thought of that attic sometimes when I heard traces of Lily's radio. She had started providing for her future, feathering her nest with resources and solutions. Mondays was late-night relationship counselling for shift workers and heartsore insomniacs. It was quite grown up; I made out the word *psychosexual*. I heard her click the radio back on after I had left her sleeping once or twice, and I wondered about going back in, but I thought it was right for her to have a secret from me. At half-term I set up a little camp bed under the window, clean sheets, my mum's old blue-and-white-striped pillow with a frill. So far neither of us had ventured into it, but it was right, I felt, that the offer was there. One night I heard Lily's self-esteem tape still running as she slept, telling her, in detail, how good and strong she was in various formations: 'I love and respect myself in my entirety. I am a girl, a woman and a goddess.' I could only agree.

Sometimes I was afraid of her seriousness and measuring. I knew she was honest and she held within her bustling thoughts, chains of words that could wound irreparably. She had every right to be hysterical, furious, brow-beaten, sad, and I knew it was my great good fortune that she was careful and mild. She was almost eerily self-contained, at times. I would have welcomed reassurance that there wasn't a reckless aspect to her caution.

One afternoon she asked to borrow a long skirt of mine, which we hitched at the back with safety pins. She found a necklace of unvarnished wooden beads. She was going to a fancy dress birthday. The theme was the person you wanted to be in ten years' time.

'What you going as?'

'I'm thinking maybe a hippy therapist?'

'Oh!'

When I woke the next morning, Lily was asleep in the little bed under the window.

I started trying harder to keep in her good books after that. It wasn't necessary, just a precautionary tactic, but there was a shift in power as she moved into her teens and I retired. I wondered how long I could keep her at my side. People haven't stuck to me particularly in life. I've dealt myself out of things, without meaning to or realising. If I started to grate on her it would not be something I could stand. I knew for all-round progress, for peace and success, the best outcome would be Eleanor becoming well enough to take over from me. That was my unspoken plan. It was what we were all hoping for, my strongest wish, when I was at my best.

EIGHT

When Lily was almost fifteen, I became unwell. She came with me to the hospital. I didn't like her to miss school, but 'It's only double maths,' she shrugged; that made me smile. We were miles early and I gave my name and bought coffees from a vending machine and lots of bleak-looking oaten biscuits because they were called Brontë. There was an exhibition mounted in white frames in the corridor – black and white photographs of hospital food through the ages: tray cloths, soup plates, starched nurses, engraved cutlery.

Lily fetched me a ribbed plastic cup of iced water. 'Would you like to sit down?' she asked, as though I were her guest.

The names of the people called before us seemed madly comical: Bea Wrigglesworth, Iona Halfhead – we couldn't stop giggling. It was defiance, in its way, rebellious schoolgirls, two bad mice. After a while an ancient-looking man came over, hovered in front of us for a moment, with that waxy thinness illness brings, no shoulders, no bottom to speak of, just trousers, good ones though, light tweed. His face was fawn-coloured, freckled, almost worn through. He addressed his speech to Lily, which surprised me.

'Your mother is very beautiful,' he said, tipping his head in my direction.

'Thank you,' she said simply.

A name was called from the nurses' station, Philip something. He drew a piece of white card from his pocket and put it in my hand. Mr and Mrs Norman J. Philips, it said, only the Mrs had been crossed out and underneath the name he had written in blue biro *RIP*. It was what passed for romance in the cancer department.

Into the doctor's little office – three other people; it was the first bad sign that I was under the care of a team. The doctor was pointlessly tall, stressed, distracted, posh English – Mr Ratcliffe. I nudged Lily: 'Let's call him Mousehill.' Her eyes lit nicely. The doctor smiled. He was performing kindly, patronising English gent, a bit sentimental and blustering. Jean would have said he was of the mould of men who somehow *knew* that women with all their feelings and whatnot didn't quite understand things rationally, weren't quite *equipped*, weren't altogether *qualified*, although let's agree they could be, in the right place, certainly on occasion, of course they could be ... *serene* ... *decorative* ... *helpful*. He looked concerned in his grey wool suit, but it was hard to know how deep it went.

'And is this ... ' he looked down at his notes, '*the lovely Lily?*' as though she were a magician's assistant, whereas in reality if she was anything she was the magician herself. The magic. She stood and took his silliness with so much intelligent dignity. She's a credit to you, Ruth, I suddenly allowed myself. That was a thought that sent out arrows of health. Mousehill shook her hand enthusiastically and it was she who finally had to end it. He wanted to be liked which was endearing in its way. I began to like him, why not? Give the people what they want.

He read my notes again and his face fell. What he had to say was evidently monstrous. The texture of his skin was emotional; the pores were of a sensitive grain and the mournful folds of his neck slumped into his shirt collar, the collar itself wanting in freshness. I noticed there was a button missing from the left sleeve of his jacket. I half wished I could sew it back on for him. Steady on.

'Shall I begin?' the senior nurse offered. She was poised and rather regal in her atmosphere. I had the reassuring sense that it was she who was really in charge. I hoped she was anyway. Mousehill nodded weakly. It was almost as though he had become the patient.

The nurse began the little bad-news bulletin. She made deft cutting movements with her hand, but she softened her voice. I could barely listen. Lily wrote fast in her rough book, as though sitting an exam.

'We usually do the major surgery on Mondays,' the nurse said.

'Oh? Will I be having major surgery?' It was quite an off-hand way of telling a person.

'That's right,' Mousehill said. 'Probably be about eleven o'clock, half past ten possibly, maybe earlier. Sometimes we begin at ten or quarter past. We'll let you know in good time, of course. So it'll be nil by mouth in any case in the morning, from five or possibly five thirty. We often say from the night before just to simplify things, really.'

He was dwelling on the barely relevant details in order to push the harsh facts to the edge of things. The whole thing was far-fetched, April Fools-ish almost. They were going to have to take out a section of my shoulder and replace it with part of my shin? That couldn't be right. I thought they were joking, like that song, your head bone's connected to your leg bone, except of course it doesn't go like that.

'Is this a procedure you've done before?'

'We do it all the time,' the nurse said.

That was something. Afterwards there might be this course of treatment or that one. The pathology would guide. Margins. Time frames. Possible new shoots. Mousehill snaked his palm this way and that into little carefree rivulets, as though to suggest how easily it would all *flow*. I switched myself off – click – closed my eyes. I would be stern, unflinching. These things could pass for brave. There was a trolley full of drugs rattling up and down the ward. I could see it making stops at all the bedsides and I imagined diving across it and grabbing great handfuls, shoving them into my mouth.

At that moment, Lily got up. 'Just going to the loo,' she said.

As soon as she was gone, I turned to the nurse, 'I'm sorry but I've got to ask, what are the chances of me not making it through the operation?'

'Let me put it another way,' Mousehill offered, bright-voiced. 'The chances of you coming through are one hundred per cent.'

'Well *that's* good.' How everybody laughed!

'And I look forward to wishing you a happy birthday when you are,' he looked down at my notes, 'seventy-five.'

OK. Five years they were giving me. Lily was nearly fifteen, a few months younger than Eleanor when she left to live with her best friend's family. I'd telephoned the mother, Cathy Loveday, the night she went. I barely knew her. I didn't know what to say. Even the punctuation in the note Eleanor left was so wounding.

'Try not to worry. These things always blow over. We're more than happy to have her here if you're happy.'

'Happy' was unfortunate. I remembered telephoning this woman a year earlier, when her daughter Laura had been sick all over our bathroom. I practised before I rang; didn't want to humiliate her. 'Hello, Cathy, Ruth here, Eleanor's mum. Hello hello. Just to say, Laura's absolutely fine and she couldn't have done it with more grace, or been more apologetic, and not a speck of anything on the rug whatsoever, but she was rather sick here last night. And she was so sweet afterwards and helpful, but I thought I should let you know.'

I hoped she would kindly remember that.

The nurse was asking if I had more questions. I would nudge Lily into adulthood but we wouldn't make twenty-one. I wouldn't be around when she had a family of her own. Or when she was making her life as a—? That was too sad, even for me. I bit down on the inside of my mouth which was sore today, the texture mottled-tasting, sour and too meaty. People don't speak of it but cancer has a taste and reek that is revolting to the sufferer. I looked down at my leg. Lily came back into the room, shyly, tactful. After seventy-five, though, there weren't really any guarantees to speak of, even if your health was –

'Can I ask something?' Lily said.

– even if your health was tip-top.

'Of course,' three voices chimed.

'How long will the surgery take?'

'Well,' Mousehill said, putting a hand to his eminent chin.

'Well,' said the young male nurse.

The chief nurse, the woman, stood. 'Fourteen to sixteen hours?'

'That's not as long as I thought,' I said quickly. 'Phew,' I added, and then a word I have only ever seen in *The Beano*, 'Phewee.' Lily would go to Jean Reynolds' for a while. They got on well; it would be thrilling for Jean. She would offer before I asked. I pictured the two of them laughing in front of the TV, huddled together on Jean's gracious sofa, picking from a plate piled high with pink cakes. Double glazing; central heating blazing; fitted carpets as far as the eye could see. I shook the image from my head.

Afterwards, on the way home, at the back of the top deck of the bus, which we had entirely to ourselves which was a luxury, Lily and I held onto each other and rocked forwards and back and I folded my arm round her and there was great heat between us and bolts of comfort fiercely exchanged and steam and snot trails and perhaps one or two tears and I felt sweat gathering under my arms, and I tried not to think of the horrible taste in my mouth. If we had spoken then it would have been to apologise to each other endlessly and then to apologise for apologising (*not at all, no no no, absolutely not, no no, nothing, not your fault in any* . . .) until there was a high tower of sorryness and of sorrow between us, in recognition that for some reason our lives were rather difficult compared to other people's. Although, of course, we were well up to it because we were strong, because we were brave and intelligent, although if we were being completely honest, it was a bit much.

That night I dreamed my illness would make Eleanor well. We had five years to get her into good shape. It was daunting. We'd not seen her for almost eight months – the three of us had had a quick cup of tea in an empty café one Sunday near Camden Lock; Lily and I shared a slice of paradise cake. In the dream there was a see-saw on a little green and I watched my figure get smaller and lighter and darker and more shrivelled while she got softer and clearer and more substantial. If I fell apart could it galvanise her somehow? That was my plan, if you could call some rigged-up, postage-stamp-sized emergency hope a plan.

Eight days before the surgery, I went to a meeting for families affected by drugs. I had discussed the possibility with Jean on

Christmas Eve. She and I were out carol singing with a few other teachers and Lily and her violin and two of her friends. Jean had about seven coats on, which made her wider than she was tall. Her short platinum hair that came in commas to her cheeks made her look moon-kissed. 'Thing is, Jean, I have done wrong and it will be my punishment,' I whispered, rattling my tambourine without much zeal, and Jean said, 'I will slap you if you ever say anything like that again. Don't forget how much you *hated* it when you went before.' But then she threw her arms round me, the only time she ever has.

'Don't let go, don't let go.' We stood there for almost a minute. 'That probably did more for my health than any surgery will,' I whispered. A tear of hers slid onto my collarbone. It might have been the cold, but for a moment I thought she might tell me she loved me, but no. My ideas were wild today. We went back to 'Good King Wenceslas'. We were tuneless but we were keen.

'It didn't end well for him,' Jean whispered.

'What are you talking about?'

'Good King Wenceslas. Done in by his brother, if you must know.'

'Was he?' Jean knew everything. 'Was he really?'

She nodded. 'Go to the meeting if you think it might help, but not because you require added torment.'

I took two buses to an old hall in Chelsea. It was Friday lunchtime and there were bells ringing and tiny children wearing lemon dresses frothing at the mouth of the church. It looked like a dance school performance or wedding rehearsal. I walked down a set of thick stone steps – the kind that would kill you if you fell. There were twenty women and two men and a kettle and flowery mugs and some biscuits spread in a ring on a shit-brown plate. I slunk in a corner for a minute or two then took a seat in a horseshoe of school chairs, dragged my chair back, metal legs rasping against dim parquet. A man was in charge, of course he was. I sat at the edge of things. Don't speak to me and don't approach me – I was trying to radiate a bit of fierceness and individuality; to convey I wasn't open to crass sympathy.

When I did hear stray phrases, accounts of doom with emphases in the strangest places – disappearing wayward sons, stolen hole-in-the-wall cards, seeing your dead mother's missing diamond ring on a blue velvet cushion in the window of the pawn shop (that was very Chelsea) – the fine details of competitive squalor, voiced like a boast, loved ones who had lost their jobs, their homes, their children, their lives, I couldn't help feeling that these people imposing fact and order on chaos were belittling themselves. I wasn't looking for friends, but the shallowness of everything dismayed me. There was cliché after cliché – expressions that couldn't help but make you think that people were vapid or not telling the whole truth, like 'emotional roller coaster', and no sentence featuring that phrase ever came to any good. I didn't seem to have any compassion. I didn't understand myself; I was usually mild in my atmosphere, mild-ish.

The central thesis of the gathering was that the best thing you could do was not to dwell unduly on your person and their trails of havoc; your job was to get on as best you could and build yourself up without them. For that I had taken two buses? You could make it clear to the addicted person they had made a series of choices you couldn't support, and so, for now, you chose not to have them in your life. But to speak of choice was a profound misunderstanding. All the other people were begging their mothers for help, handouts, hope, approval, cash or assorted crumbs of those things. Eleanor didn't want us in her life. She'd turned us away.

I despised the other women in the room and their complacency. Utterly defeated people. How they could call the pamphlets they handed round and sold from a side table 'literature'! They all believed acceptance was the answer. Human stodge they were, brainless, paralysed, jargon-spouting and robotic in their cheery print dresses and tightened lips. I saw the worst of myself in the gathered crowd. It was so ugly to me. I was.

The woman next to me was talking about the death of her son. On and on she went, voice like a demented headstone. I didn't need things like that. I wondered what I might say if I spoke. 'We are all at peace now,' she said. 'It is over. I am hugely grateful for that.'

I wanted to hit her. She was inhuman.

I could try something myself. I rehearsed a few lines in my head: *My daughter cannot or will not be a mother to her child. The volume of shame, grief and despair this causes me is inexpressible. I hope one day things will change. I have cancer now. So . . . so it's our last chance.*

I raised my hand to speak and the leader nodded his permission. I opened my mouth a little. My voice cracked slightly and I heard it announce to the room, 'I cannot bear it that she doesn't want to be daughters with me.' Then all I could hear were racking sobs in the air, stabbing the ghostly echoes of wedding music from the church above. I felt my skin redden, my head shaking from side to side, scatterings of disgrace. I sensed the arch disdain and embarrassment of the other people travelling through my body. No one even reached out a hand. People said love and work were the strongest things in life, but I wondered if it was truer to say work and grief.

I turned my back on the meeting and swiftly climbed the steps to daylight. I fought my way through the brightly coloured wedding party that was emerging. Church bells exploded in the air above me. Suddenly I was face to face with the bride in her lace dress, who looked no older than one of my sixth-form girls. She was radiant and trembling with sprigs of waxy orange blossom on a little crown in her hair. I worried my tears might cause her distress, but perhaps she would take them for tears of joy. I could not think what to express to her so I just flashed her a double thumbs-up! On the bus home I brushed flakes of confetti off my lapels; picked rice out of my fringe. I wished Eleanor could fall in love.

When I got home, Lily was back from school already, cleaning out the fridge determinedly. There was something about a child in a school uniform and an apron and rubber gloves wielding a J-cloth that looked very humorous.

'My hero!' I greeted her.

She grinned. 'Eleanor's coming over.' She spoke casually. 'So ...'

'Oh? Coming here? Today?' She hadn't been to the flat for several years.

'She didn't sound too bad on the phone. She wants to help us, I think. That's what she said. She said, "What can I do?" I wanted to let her know about the operation. Thought she ought to know. That it was right. She said she would be over shortly.'

'You just rang?'

'Yeah. I would want to know in her place. If it was me.'

'Oh, I see. Oh good! Of course. How thoughtful. Thank you so much.'

'Have a sit-down,' she said. 'I've made you some green tea. I got it at the health food shop. It's very healing, according to the box. Although I suppose they would say that, wouldn't they. Was on special offer, though, forty per cent off.'

'Bargain. I could get used to this.'

'I spoke to the woman there.'

'The larger lady? Tessa?'

'Yes. She asked if I wanted a hug!'

'Did she? Did you?'

'Oh, and she said we should lay off the dairy products. In her opinion.'

It was tempting to say 'Well she can talk!' but I rose above it.

'Do you think she's going to be hungry, Eleanor?' Lily asked me.

'I wonder.'

'What time is it?'

'Four thirty-seven.'

'OK.'

'And she sounded . . . ?'

'Ye-ah. I think so. Quite sort of, I don't know, businesslike? If that makes sense.'

'Oh well, that's good.'

'Should I maybe make a cake or something? I think we've got the stuff. I mean, it's quite a special . . . '

'What d'you think?'

'We did one at school last week, lemon and coconut. It was pretty good.' She went into her room and came back with a yellow folder. She drew out a printed sheet and read it through, then started measuring things into little bowls: sugar, butter, flour. I loved the rigour of her.

'She's probably not going to come, though,' she was saying now.

'Well, there is that.'

'Think I'll leave it.' She tipped the sifted flour carefully back into the packet, folded down the blue and white edges three times, spooned the sugar back into the enamel storage jar, lifted the butter proud onto a knife and wedged it back against the block. She washed and dried the dishes, put them away.

'You're so lovely and sensible,' I said.

She rolled her eyes – a healthy gesture.

She got out her homework. Somehow she managed to have two or three hours' worth every evening, had done for years. Her drive unsettled me, although it had my admiration. I worried it was disproportionate, a show of strength in some way misapplied. It was a kind of courage, I suppose, a moral energy, but I felt it was a false equation she was answering, because she gave so much more than was necessary. I wished she had a lighter tone to herself now and then, but I respected her choices. It was not cosmetic the way she organised herself. It went deep. She went deep. Still, there may have been a hint of reproach intended for me.

I knew teachers didn't always warm to the hard-working pupils as much as they might. Like the rest of the world they were drawn to the happy-go-lucky and the easy-going, the carefree girls who chattered and scoffed. They were influenced by looks and playful light-heartedness, even though they – we – didn't care to admit it. A little-known fact was that teachers were sometimes embarrassed by the overtly conscientious. I'd been guilty of this myself. The desire to please us that these girls carried could make for awkward-ness and claustrophobia. It was too intimate, too loaded. They wanted things from us – attention, validation, approval – that they should have been getting from home. I worried sometimes that Lily gave in her homework as though bestowing a tremendous gift, which would be lost on a mark scheme that hadn't room for an answer ranging so far beyond the modest demands of the ques-tions. Occasionally Jean passed on praise for Lily that she gathered from colleagues in the staffroom. For her faultless work and her endearing personality. No one complained of a heaviness, but they mentioned how lively she was. A pleasure to teach. I worried too much possibly.

Eleanor didn't show, but we had a nice evening playing rummy and we found some crumbly fudge to gamble with at the back of the fridge. It felt like a celebration: Lily's long pink arms shuffling the deck with a lot of finesse; the brightness of the diamonds and the hearts. The tea we drank was powdery and soothing. Illness heightened everything. I placed a higher value on my surroundings. I thought of the part of pregnancy two thirds of the way through, before exhaustion set in, when the world was crammed with hope and promise: the greens of trees dazzled with bright vegetable freshness; the lines on the face of the newspaper seller on the corner, framed by feverish headlines, looked like poetry; the red of a double-decker bus so saturated and optimistic – even if it was the wrong number. I thought often these days of my mother clinging onto life so she could witness Lily's arrival. She had always exerted a great deal of effort in trying to stay alive. It didn't come naturally.

'I'm sorry Eleanor didn't make it,' Lily said at bedtime.

'Well – I had a lovely time.'

'Yeah.'

'Do you, do you ever feel, Lil, that you'd like us to talk about her more?'

'Would *you* like us to?'

'If you would.'

'Do you think about her much?'

'I *feel* her all the time. But it's been going on for so long that I suppose I sometimes try to push it to the edge of my mind.'

'Do you think that's what I should do?' she asked.

'Not necessarily.'

'Do you think she's happy?'

'Well – she's *busy*. She has a passion of sorts that defines her day. So each day would have purpose, and she has friends who live in the same way who sort of plan things and then relax together, so she certainly would have good times, where she would feel safe and sort of mellow. I hope. A bit floppy, maybe, like when you've worked really hard and look forward to a lovely rest. But I wonder if it gets her down that she doesn't use her talents more, isn't able to express herself in that way, because she's clever and she could really do something amazing if she . . . Hard to say. Hard to say I suppose what makes a happy life.'

She smiled. 'I'm reading this book at the moment about mothers who are estranged from their children.'

'Are you? Where d'you find that?'

'It's very sad.'

'Can you tell me about it?'

'I don't want to upset you.'

'I can take it. Might be helpful.'

'Because you're estranged from your daughter too?'

I nodded.

'I'm the only person in this family who isn't estranged from her daughter,' Lily suddenly cried. 'What chance has she got?'

'Lily, darling, I—'

'Sorry, sorry, sorry.' She recovered herself quickly. 'I mean, I'm being stupid! I don't even have a daughter, do I?'

'Well, there is that, I suppose.' I picked up her hand and kissed the back of it. She got into bed beside me.

'There's so much pressure,' she said.

'Yes, there is.'

'It, it talks about shame a lot in the book, actually.'

'Does it? What does it say?'

'I wrote it down. Hang on a sec.' She reached for her school bag and pulled out her rough book. 'It says, "Shame cuts us off from receiving love from a partner or friends or family" and "Shame separates us from others because it feels incommunicable and so we have to hide important parts of ourselves."'

I nodded.

'What do you think?'

'Well, I can see why someone might think those things, have those beliefs.' I was breathing carefully. It was a conversation I did not know how to have.

'One of the saddest things in the book was when a woman's husband made her leave the family home because, I don't remember why, and she was allowed to visit every other Sunday for a hundred minutes, and one day, on one of the visits, her daughter said to her, "Mum, I wish I could divorce you too."'

'Oh dear.'

'SO harsh.'

'Yes, that is harsh. Although . . . '

'The book said that being a mother apart from your child left most people with deep scars.'

'The children, you mean?'

'No, the mothers.'

'Oh. Where did you find this book?'

'It was on sale in the health food shop, by the till. The lady said I could borrow it if I read it carefully so she could still sell it.'

'Oh, I see.'

'It was next to the manuka honey.'

'Is that the really expensive one?'

'Yeah.' She looked away from me. 'Do you think Eleanor is still in touch with my dad?'

'My feeling is not, but we could ask?'

'Maybe.'

'Will you read on, do you think? Would you like us to look at it together?'

'Not sure.'

'OK. See how you go. No rush.'

She thought for a moment. 'You know, I'll always be so grateful for everything you've done for me.'

I smiled, kissed her head, climbed out of bed, left the room. I started to cry uncontrollably. I shut myself in the bathroom so she could not hear. I had such an overwhelming urge to harm myself, what was left of me. Thanking me for bringing her up. Christ, what a terrible thing to say. I stood shaking, leaning against the basin, watching my despair mounting in the mirror. I found one of the yellow pills prescribed for anguish by Mousehill, broke it in half, took both pieces. 'Everyone gets a touch of it now and then going through this,' he reassured me. 'Anxiety and depression do seem to creep in with this disease, I'm afraid. Can't be helped. I am sorry about that.'

I looked at him, incredulous. 'I've had anxiety and depression all my life!'

It would take a little while for the pill to kick in. I talked to myself like a baby, a cooing and soothing cow-dove soundtrack, but the baby only roared.

I saw Luke in Lily's eyes suddenly. It was a shock to me. I'd not seen that before. It was something cold I identified; not cold exactly, more the sense of imbalance that naturally occurs when you look to someone for something important and it skews all the proportions, makes the other person very big while you scarcely register for them at all.

I slept with Luke five times that summer. I remember each one distinctly. What he wore, what was eaten afterwards (or before). The thick sky – the heat that August was full of dust – another time the sky completely colourless, unreal, all day heavy cloud, weary and swollen, and then when it broke and everything at four o'clock went charcoal grey before thunder and a furious storm. His distracted air, his prowling summer boredom – Christine was at her mother's with the children; it was a couple of years after they had split – and there was the sense that he wasn't living deliberately somehow. His giddy incredulity that I would go along with it, when I had such long-standing ties to his wife from our school days. He was scorched by my betrayal of her. It made me more valuable without doubt, although I had not seen her for a few years, as with her boys and a small amount of time for work she found no room for my friendship. That was a little painful, you could say. His brief indecipherable mutterings I remember, an odd sense that there was in the air a kind of sportsmanship involved, in place of romance. What began as astonishment moved into something more like a light irony. Two lonely people in the broiling city, emptied of reality.

One evening I met a friend and Luke was in the group with someone else, and one by one they left and then it was just him and me, and he held a match to a cork from the bottle we were drinking and let it char and cool and then he drew beards and moustaches on us. That was how it began. His hand on the side of my face, drawing things, the dry drag and brush of the cork. Russian-looking beards he gave us, matching, with curlicues and pointed tips. Were we meant to be clowns? Surrealist painters? I told him he looked like Tolstoy. Tolstoy by Picasso maybe, seated, with a top hat by his side. That made him smile. I could barely see him in the flickering candlelight. He said my eyes were like shy stars.

'But there's no such thing!'

'That's what *you* think.' The bitter taste of charcoal sharpened my senses.

I don't know why I did it. I wasn't very alive during that time and he seemed to have terrific life bouncing off him and I wanted some of it. I was in a kind of trance. My mother was dying – she was already unwell, and then she got pneumonia – and it was the school holidays so there was no work, and I spent my days with her, trying to hold on to her life. Things had often been difficult for her and I was determined death wouldn't be. I was still trying to compensate her for all she had suffered in her youth. Of course, when you looked after someone at the end of things you learned more about what it meant to die than a living person should know. The shock and wounds of it went into your tissue, X-rays of dismay, the body's final needs; and the outrage that it could be happening and the shame that you couldn't stop it, your powerlessness, and then you ended up cursing because you realised one of the chief facts about life is that you cannot prevent anything at all. Then seeing someone fade almost to nothing, the skin stretched, trans-lucent parchment, bones visible, hair blanching as if the strands themselves were in a state of shock. It took a long time to forget scenes like that. Perhaps you never did. That was all, at first.

It wasn't domestic with him. There wasn't much in the way of smiling or cake crumbs, it was businesslike. There was a straight-ness. Everything was as it seemed. I had a sense he would have fled from any show of gratitude. I think he wanted to believe I had to break with myself in some profound way to do it. He didn't realise that the prospect of my mother dying was already so shattering to my sense of self, nothing else had much solidity. Still, it took care of some of the pain.

The miracle was she came through the pneumonia; we were none of us expecting that. 'So little but so much fight in her,' the doctor said. She had situated herself in a higher category than he had placed her. A robust family, he judged. That delighted me. Perhaps I did revive her in my way, if that is possible, some of the life force spilling onto her, the high voltage of my mad nights fuelling her resistance and my desire. I made soup for her every afternoon in her flat. Heat, tears, vegetable hope, that early part of mourning when the person hasn't died yet and you feel a bit more alive than you can take because stocks are in short supply. Doomed elation: everything concentrated and electric. And of course you started thinking mad things like if only this soup could be the best soup in the history of soup you might just win; if you chopped the onion, celery and carrot into fairy dice and walked two miles each way to the market with heavy bags because the spinach there was the greenest you had ever seen, and cheap. If you grated a bit of your thumb into the pan with the nutmeg. Very good soup could keep people alive. Mine did. There was proof – she went on living for the best part of a year. It was a small miracle. I was able to touch Eleanor's fingers and toes to her a few times right at the start, right at the end. In a strange sort of way when you were tired and squinting they looked almost the same. Perhaps that was what she kept going for. I did get a sense of the completion of things.

He liked to put a record on sometimes: Miles Davis, Duke Ellington. Once he brought two bottles of champagne and we were lavishly drunk. It was the fourth time and that was more carefree. He was wearing a checked shirt. I allowed myself on that occasion to admire his muscular limbs, his broad shoulders, all that. He didn't do it often, but when he smiled there was a sense of sunlight and repair. Afterwards we slept lumpily against each other for eight hours solid. His face was friendly in the morning under startled-looking hair. I put out a hand to smooth it down. I sensed his admiration of me growing. We both drank great pint mugs of tea and I made eggs before I went off to my mum's. He liked me very light about everything, smiling, mild opinions, carefree. But beneath that he wanted me tender in my personality; it was how a woman should be, with intelligent courage, a careful imagination for the difficulties of others, soft laughter, delicate feminine instincts. A sense of duty. If you think of the way a doctor sometimes says with sympathy as he presses against you with his fingers, 'Is it tender here?' Like that. He could overlook a certain sadness as long as it wasn't twee, but anger would have struck him as unsightly. In a way he was like a little child who had always been lionised.

I hoped it might tip over into something. Twice a month, could he run to that, just pop in to see me, brusquely if needs be, even to have a cup of tea and just a friendly chat if that was—? Once a month? I knew it wasn't right to ask for anything. I might have loved him. A few times a year? For him the fascination was at first, I think, that he had thought better of me. He was shocked. How the mighty have fallen! And then when Christine came back from her mother's we largely kept our distance even though they weren't together any more. Caring for my mother with a baby growing inside me did make losing her a bit easier. It made her happy also. These were not small things.

There had been one moment of high romance between us, or something resembling it. How it went was that I telephoned him late one night. I had spent all day trying not to and all day knowing that I would. The evening had an odd texture to it already, the sky still bright at nine o'clock and almost no cloud or wind, but an odd sense of pressure building. I was waiting for my mother to fall asleep and then I waited for her to be sleeping deeply. She had had her soup and her egg custard and all her various medicines.

'Hello there,' he said. He was bored, I expect, possibly a little drunk, and although he didn't often bother with charm – he didn't need to – he did that night. I heard him pour a drink and take a drag on a cigarette. I remember there was some sort of joking from his side that all good things came in threes and I was the third thing, which made me laugh because everyone knows it is catastrophes that are meant to arrive three at a time. There was a big smile in his voice as if the fact of me, the fact of me piercing his evening late at night, was a bit de luxe. That he was in the mood for feminine company. I thought he might request or demand a reason or excuse for my call but he didn't. It was good timing. We spoke lightly for a few minutes about I don't know what. Then:

'Are you happy in your life?' he asked.

I closed my eyes. I had the oddest sensation in that moment when I was talking to him that I was very happy, not only happier than I'd ever been but happier than anyone had ever been. I told him so and I felt he saw me properly that night for the first time, even though we were only on the phone. He liked my saying that very much. When people expected you to drone on about sadness, saying you felt wonderful could make them really love you.

At the end of the phone call I was sure he would come and live with me. It was what he wanted in his heart but there was a thick net of things that had to be worked through first, and that would take time and I must be patient. That, and grow up a bit for him, I got the feeling. It was clear in any case that he was ready for domestic life again. He missed it. A mooring. I almost told him about the coming baby but I didn't want to spoil things when it was all going so well. My mother had a bad night but it barely grieved me. All the next day I was in a wild dream.

We met in dribs and drabs after Eleanor was born, until she was two and he closed things down. I sometimes remembered the form I had signed saying I would expect nothing further from him in exchange for the money and the little picture. He had given all he would give and he wanted his privacy. Before that time I was always waiting. His footsteps when they came were almost silent on the stairs. Soft knocking on the door late at night, unannounced. Always when things were quiet for him elsewhere. He was often impatient when he dropped in, as though I had kept him waiting or looked him up at an inconvenient time. Restless. Still I was shy with him, in awe of him a little bit. Once he brought a watermelon and he halved it with one swipe, using a bread knife like a sword, and we ate thick cool chunks of it in bed, laughing, spitting the pips, to hell with the mess.

When he descended on me out of the blue, high and free, I saw the compliment of it. I thought of him as a long-lost relation. A sailor coming into port – agitated, sweat on his brow – who needed somewhere calm to lay his head. He was good company. And it was hard for me to feel I was stealing from anyone when there was so much loss in the air.

NINE

I was narrowing things; closing it all down. I spent days going through bits of paper. Bits of myself. There were letters from Eleanor that had to be burned. Unsent things from me to my father I had no memory of writing, so strange, from forty years ago – fierce ghost correspondence, didn't even sound like me. When did I learn the more you wanted from people, the less they gave? Early on. I lit a match and watched the blue flame dart and leap across the thin sheets covered in black biro imprecations. I felt like an old lady in an American novella, flummoxing impertinent biographers; the wry finale: extinction, revenge. Up they went! The paper blackened and crumbled. Charred fragments floating wayward in the air. It was oddly powerful, burning things. I could see why people got a taste for it. Still, it was lonely, private work; a lawless response to intolerable emotion.

There was a kebab house near where we lived, a family-run place very warm from the grill at the back of the long oblong room and from the heart of the Greek woman, Lena, who owned and man-aged it. I wandered up there. It was the perfect place to go after a day spent destroying things. Lena was standing in the doorway, protective, benevolent. She held out her arms. She had a tremendous atmosphere of courage. It might have been all that time spent in proximity to hot coals.

I let her envelop me. I breathed her in, charred meat, rose water, oregano, freckled pillow flesh. I had the sense I was forgiven. Lena knew Eleanor when she was little, serving me huge breastfeeder's portions when I went in starving on the Saturday afternoons after my mother died. I was the only person I ever heard of whom grief made ravenous. I wheeled the pram up the three shallow steps, hoping the smell of the food on the grill would not wake the baby. I always had the same thing at the corner table, the special offer: cubes of lamb, burnt on the outside, rosy at their middles, with chips and rice and pitta bread and smoky onions and chopped salad and yoghurt and cucumber, and a cup of English tea. Kept me going for a couple of days then. I was eating for three.

Lena knew Lily too. She gave her purple lollipops in cellophane wrappers, and she knew about me, that I was not right in my life. She was very respectful of people's pain, honouring the fact of it whilst retaining an incurious stance.

I felt wet where my arm met my neck. Lena had started to cry, literally on my shoulder. I was glad she felt she could, in some ways. Her husband Dimitri sat in a chair by the till under a grey Anglepoise, writing figures in neat columns in a hard-backed notebook, his face creased and stricken in the shadows, while she kept the spirits of the restaurant buoyant. I sometimes thought they were one person split in two. Their tragedy was that their son had died three years ago. He just didn't wake up one night, one morning. Forty-two he was, not ill in any way, a mystery, sudden adult death syndrome it said in the local paper. A whole branch of their life over, the main branch. I went to the funeral; queued for almost an hour at the end to bend and kiss the coffin. I was glad to see he had been popular: streams of beautiful girls in beautiful clothes.

I knew that every day on the way into work they dropped in at the cemetery to see how he was doing. People don't stop living just because they are dead, not entirely. You still need to love them, worry about them, console them, cheer them, humour them. Tell them when they're wrong. If Eleanor died – I understood prayers for the dead more than anything else religion offered.

Lena's crying was getting stronger. There was something about me that made it possible for her. We were magnets for each other's hidden sorrow. She could smell the cancer possibly. As more time passed since she had lost her son and the shock diminished, her dismay came through more powerfully. She gave up hoping for a reprieve. This was it now. Still, the restaurant thrived. The atmosphere of grief was unmistakable, but sad people needed a place where they could go to enjoy themselves. The food was designed to comfort and soothe. A good square meal on an oval plate was almost biblical, from some angles. They were a religious family, Greek Orthodox. That helped to a degree.

If it was a little bit disgusting of me to collect the mothers of dead children, I wasn't going to apologise. These people have naturally come to lean on me, spotting some fellow feeling, sharp clashes of shame and wounded pride; for it is the mother's most basic duty, the lowest rung – isn't it? – to keep her child alive. In the dry cleaner's there was a woman, Miss Alex, whose son, Ravi, was killed in an accident at work. Thirty-eight, a father of three, a model citizen, she said, which always made us both laugh, as though he was an Action Man or something, an enthusiast for men's leisure jewellery and cable crew-neck knitwear (dry clean only). The other grandmother hogged the kids, that was the worst part, in reality. In the downstairs flat at our old place in Brownswood Road there was a very brittle woman renting for a while who had lost her baby daughter Celeste; insisted she would never recover. It was the only thing that frightened her. She loathed the daughters of her friends, indulged in ogreish scowling at small children in the street, poor cheated soul. Her husband gently urged her to try to think of what she had instead of what she lacked. It was tempting to kill him, *yes*, she said.

I sat down at a table at Lena's – I couldn't eat this kind of food any more, but the waiter with the bad back came over stiffly and I ordered two dips that I could lick from a spoon. It was Lena's company I craved. She came and sat down with me, something she never usually did, but it was quiet – a Monday. This was a great honour.

'I need to tell you something. I'm not well. I may not be much longer for this world.' It felt as though I was offering my resignation.

'No!' she cried. 'You crazy, Ruthie darling.' She always called me that.

I nodded my head. 'It's true.' I spoke carefully. I saw my words go in and a small flicker of panic in her eyes. She looked at me with great awe then and cried a little more and then she kissed me on my forehead as though she were a priest in her long skirts, or even the Pope, and her eyes communicated to me firm and absolute in their belief that I had been blessed. I saw that she envied me.

The cancer got the better of me quickly. I couldn't walk more than a few yards without fighting for breath. The operation was like a horror film. The recovery process slow and agonising. I wasn't able to give a good account of myself. All I could think was that I wanted it to stop. They kept me in for five weeks – almost double what they'd said. The effort of keeping a bit up for Lily lifted my spirits, although it may have made the pain worse. The nerve strain and the nausea, I had heard, were more acute if you fought. The line of the scar I was aware of all the time; you could see the purplish stitch marks, the surrounding skin puckered and angry, the sort of bad seam your needlework teacher would make you unpick and redo. I felt any sharp movement would rip me open. It was indescribable the sense that your head was uncertainly attached. My face pulled against itself, angry, sunken, horribly lopsided, the red crack glowing like a curse, flesh dragging on the bone, the features poorly arranged. And then one day I could not pretend any more. Lily saw things she should not have seen; she witnessed my despair. Perhaps there was a small element of relief on both sides. I had been protecting her from it all her life, in any case.

She was brilliant when she got me home after the operation, cheerful, careful. Jean came in the morning before work each day and again in the evening, bringing food and flowers, beautiful books. A hot breakfast for Lily on a flowery plate, and on her birthday pancakes with wild blueberry compote and a canister of squirty cream. Three fifty-pound notes! Lily yelped with joy. The care they put into me, night and day, Lily sleeping in an armchair in my room, without complaint: 'Oh, it's so cosy!' Nights and nights in a row reading to me, both at home and at the hospital, massaging my swollen legs, which looked like something from the discount meat market on Seven Sisters Road, chatting gently on soothing subjects, performing being completely all right round the clock, so well that it did seem true. I was oddly contented when I didn't think about things. It was solid attention like I had never known. It made me well in every way – apart from my health.

Then the treatment began and I couldn't tolerate it. It struck like extreme sunburn on the inside of my body. My neck and chest cratered and there were lurid sores to contend with, splayed marks like wine-coloured rot. Quite something to retch when you glimpsed yourself in a dark window at night. The misery I wasn't equal to, the ripping feeling when I breathed. That I was wounded so visibly was a source of deep shame. It seemed to prove something about me I had all my life hoped wasn't true. I lost my nerve, had to stop the treatment. The doctors were appalled. I tried again, but my limbs jerked and shook uncontrollably, aping a mad seizure, and between us all we could not get me to be still. I was unable to help myself. Then I tried a third time, my morale too low to protest, but still it was more than I could endure. 'Time is what we don't have,' Mousehill said to me, the lovely regal nurse nodding at his side. It was in my bones now. I heard myself apologise. Mousehill shed a tear and the nurse gave him her hanky. Sometimes I wondered if they were my mother and father.

'I have used up all my stock of courage in life,' I told them calmly at the hospital one afternoon. 'There isn't any left.'

A few weeks later I tried the treatment again as an inpatient. They had to drug me to get me to agree, but I agreed to the drugs; at least I think I did. Lily and Jean signed something. Half a little yellow pill quarter of an hour before and the other half after as a reward. They wheeled me down to the basement from the top floor. Sang me silly songs, the two of them, as the lift made its effortful descent. In the polished steel I looked so grey and shrivelled. They put me on to the machine, fixed me down, clamped me in. I felt like I was going to be electrocuted for past crimes.

Constant infections meant we had to stop again and start again and stop again – I seemed to keep ruining everything. More meetings, more tests, more intravenous antibiotics. The scars on my hand from the cannulae made me gag. I'd always quite liked my hands and now they were fucked.

One afternoon the doctor berated me for not being serious about my treatment. 'You don't know what you're doing!' he shouted. Very quietly Lily got out of the chair next to my bed and stood up to him. 'I hope, Mr Ratcliffe, in all your life,' she said, 'that no one *ever* speaks to your mother as you have just spoken to my – to mine.' She sat down. Put her hands in her lap.

'Well she needs to—' the doctor began harshly, but then he stopped himself, hung his head. 'I am sorry,' he mumbled. 'Wrong of me.'

It was one of the best moments of my life.

You made that, I said to myself.

On the ward, between treatments, time went more slowly than was decent. I watched the hands of the clock mark each minute. I wasn't happy that Lily skipped school to stay with me, but she wouldn't hear of anyone else. She was living between Jean's and the hospital now, a backpack of books gently swinging from her shoulder. Jean brought me in an endless supply of fresh white cotton pin-tucked nighties, socks and pants for Lily, T-shirts and jumpers, everything beautifully ironed. Lily was very careful with me, that was another great gift she had. I had.

When half-term came Jean did some of the appointments. She told me what a credit to me Lily was, how lovely it was getting to know her a bit better. I could not bring myself to thank her. It was in my liver now. They said the treatment was more likely to take if you had a companion with you. Life punished the lonely at every turn. They were no longer trying to cure me, just to tide me over for a bit, something like that. Jean's daughter came down on the train and did one of the sessions when Jean and Lily caught colds. Such a plain girl.

One day I wanted to see a priest.

The nurse said she could get me one at five o'clock. He came onto the ward at ten to five, footsteps light and springy, and – amazing this – he brought me a bunch of fancy pale daffodils with orange coronas. I nearly burst into tears. 'Depression is to me what Wordsworth was to daffodils,' I said to him. He smiled and I tried to return it. 'I'm not even a believer,' I said.

'Nobody's perfect,' he answered. 'Have you seen the state of my church? I have to say sorry before I open my mouth to speak these days. But you didn't ask me here for an act of contrition.'

'That's true. It's very, it's very democratic of you to make me one.'

'I don't have any illusions about myself,' he said.

'No. Nor have I.'

He was peering at me weirdly. 'Oh, but we've met before! About fifteen years ago. Do you remember? In Upper Holloway, was it, or was it when I was still at Our Lady? I baptised your little granddaughter.'

'Oh!'

'And now here we are . . . '

'I thought you looked familiar. I remember you now. I'm sorry I look so rough.'

'You look grand.'

I tried to shake my head. He was smiling. 'Soup and sonatas, wasn't it?'

'That's me all right,' he chuckled.

We were both amazed.

'So, how have you been?' He laughed at the mad breadth of the question.

'Um ...' I said.

'I had such high hopes for everything that day, but then I had an awful feeling I was making everything worse. I was out of my depth. I don't tend to see obstacles in life. I made up my mind not to when I was a kid. It's a sort of blindness I have.'

'You were absolutely marvellous. Holding the baby and everything. All your kindness.'

'Is your daughter ... may I ask?'

For a second I felt like saying to him, 'All is well. Turned her life around. Unrecognisable. Great teacher, great daughter, great mum,' as though it was he who was dying.

'She's still with us,' I said. 'She's, she's a work in progress, you could say.'

'I hear you. Can't be easy.'

'Well ...'

'I'll hold her in my prayers, unless that would offend you.'

'No, no. I'd like that.'

'And the little one? She all right, all right-ish?'

'She's brilliant,' I said. 'Clever, kind, thoughtful. Been looking after me so nicely. I'm very lucky. She'll be here in a minute. She comes every day after school.'

He smiled and nodded.

We sat there in silence for a minute or two.

'Thank you for being here.'

He smiled and nodded again.

'The things I want to say are very hard.'

'Are they?'

I blinked.

'It can be hard to say the things that mean a great deal to us.'

'Yes.'

'Do you think you might feel better afterwards? I'm not saying you *would* feel better. You yourself know best how your heart works.'

'Sometimes it's better to try and forget sad things.'

'It can be, yes.'

'I've made a lot of mistakes in my life.'

'Have you? Thank you for telling me that.'

I half laughed.

After a while he said, 'May I have your hand?'

I smiled for a second because it sounded like a marriage proposal. I moved my hand towards his on the bed cover. I had the sense he was trying to come up with something absolutely amazing to say. I felt his fingers on my fingers.

'I'm very tired,' I said.

'Of course. You must be absolutely exhausted.'

'And I am so sad about some things.'

'Yes. The sadness of life can be overwhelming at the best of times.'

'Yes, it can.'

'Peace will come. It will come,' he said. 'I'm sure of it.'

'Are you?'

He nodded.

'I'm not so sure.'

He smiled.

'Sometimes I think there was something about loving my own child that provoked fury in the part of me that had gone unloved myself.'

'Ah,' he said. And then, 'I think I understand.'

'Do you?'

'Let me share it with you,' he said, his voice so soft. 'Hand it over to me. Let the feeling travel across your shoulders and down your arm and through your fingertips and into my safe keeping.'

'Thank you.'

'Everybody has difficult feelings to manage some of the time. It's part of what life is. I'm sure you were better than you know. You were wonderful on the day of the christening. I remember thinking that woman's a bloody saint. SO much dignity you had. And kindness like you wouldn't believe, which is faith in pure form.'

'That is very good of you.' I had started to cry but I was laughing too, the tears like nettles on my terrible skin.

'You know, you probably saved the little one's life.'

'I don't know about that. Possibly.'

'I would say so.'

'But who has she got now?'

He was really thinking hard. 'What would you like to see happen now you are entering this new phase of life?'

'I don't know.'

'Can you forgive yourself?'

'I don't know how.'

'As you would forgive a dear friend who was suffering?'

'Maybe, I'm not sure.'

'Because I know for a fact you are forgiven by the highest judge, who loves you and admires you.'

'I don't think I can believe that.'

'With your permission now I would like to say a few prayers for—'

Lily walked in at that moment, alert-looking, lips parted in readiness, with everything to give. I felt great pride. It was as though the sun was advancing all the way along the ward. I started to cry. I hid my face.

'Shall I come back in ten minutes?' she said.

The priest looked to me. I was too tired to speak any more, but I just raised my right thumb.

'I'll get a Twix from the machine. I always have a Twix on Fridays.'

The priest held out a pound coin. 'Have it on me.

'May the Lord bless you and keep you and make his face to shine upon you . . . '

'Was I dreaming?' I asked her later on.

'When do you mean?'

'When that man was here, the one from your wedding. Did you recognise him?'

'I'm not sure I did,' Lily said. 'I am not sure.'

'He was sitting here on the bed with me.'

'Oh,' she said. 'OK. Sounds lovely. Let me lie down next to you and we'll try to get some sleep. It's going to be a beautiful day tomorrow, apparently, nineteen degrees and no clouds.'

Lily got Eleanor in to see me. I don't know how. I knew I was near the end then. Got Eleanor to say she loved me, that she was doing so much better now and would be a good mum to Lily and that I had been a good mum all on my own with hardly any support from anyone and she loved and respected me greatly, as a single mother and also professionally. Her friends at school loved me for what I had done for them, she said, Holly, Zoe, Sheila, my belief in their confidence, and that I had done everything right, and that she and Lily would be a team against the world together now and Lily was so clever nothing would stop her being anything she wanted in life, a surgeon or prime minister or a supermodel, it was all hers for the taking. She promised me she was better than ever and that Lily would be all right always too, her children and her grandchildren even she would take good care of. I didn't know what to believe but she did look better. She held my hand and her face was brimming. That sharpness in her mouth had gone down, the hard cords in her neck and her pinched eyes. She didn't look wintry. She said I was brave. All my life I have wanted someone to say that to me. It was like a dream sequence in a black and white film, coloured by memory.

'I am sorry, Mum,' she told me when she said goodbye.

'You have absolutely nothing to be sorry for.'

She loved me so much and I loved her.

'How can she be better?' I asked Lily when she had gone and I didn't know what to believe.

'She is better,' Lily said. 'Not completely, but a definite improvement. She's been having treatment, not residential, but it's made a real difference.'

'Are you telling me the truth?'

'She gets small amounts of methadone from the doctor every day, maybe every other day. She's on a scheme. They have counselling and everything. It's really helped her stabilise. And she's been working at a centre for homeless people near Aldgate station, a day centre. She does the lunches in a stripy apron and they have a sing-along on Tuesday afternoons after the chiropodist comes, she said. One of the volunteers plays the guitar. In the waiting room she was reading *Villette*. That's got to be a good sign.'

'*Villette*?'

Lily nodded.

'I love that one. The people in the school were so severe.'

'I know ... and the way the headmistress spies on her, going through all her stuff like that. Gave me such a massive shock!'

Oh yes.

She smiled and moved her chair in a little bit.

'I know you don't want to leave us,' she whispered. I grasped her hands. 'But I promise you we will be fine always. We're going to look after each other. We've made a plan. There is nothing for you to worry about ever. Just rest now. All the love in the world.'

I wanted it to be true so much it *was* true. Sometimes in life you have to let your heart and bones off the hook of yourself. I could hardly speak from that point.

Lily traced the shape of a heart on my hand. I felt myself slip into a state of mourning.

TEN

I had to get Eleanor to the hospital. We had three days, four days. I wanted everything perfect. I was concentrating all the time. I dreamed I got the bus over there, broke down the door, forced my way in. I stepped over random sleeping bodies until I found her, made her drink a cup of coffee, made her eat a cream cheese sandwich that I brought. 'Listen to me, Eleanor.' I spoke clearly and slowly. 'I have never asked you anything but I am asking you now. You are going to have a wash, you're going to put on your best clothes and you are coming with me to the hospital to say goodbye to your mother. It's your last chance to do the right thing.' My hands shook. My voice was metal.

Some guy came into the room, tall and shadowy, gross dirty grey sweatpants with nothing on top. Skin and bone. Was it maybe like my dad? 'Hey, people are sleeping!' he protested. That was when I went mad. It was the idea that I didn't know how to behave. He was shocked and took a backwards step and pulled a face that said, 'Hey, you are hurting my feelings.' Jesus. By the time I finished with him, Eleanor had drifted off to sleep again. And then I did something I shouldn't have done (even in my dreams). I went into the kitchen, found a cup that wasn't completely covered with all sorts of filth and I filled it with cold water and I went back into the bedroom and I flung it in her face.

Of course, it wasn't like that. I did go round there, though. I rang the bell and waited on the doorstep for ages. In the end I wrote out a card I bought at the shop on the corner. It had a picture of the Queen in a yellow coat holding flowers. *Hi Eleanor, I hope you're well. Ruth is very ill in hospital. I'm afraid she doesn't have long. Please come as soon as you can.* I put the hospital address and the phone number and the floor and the name of the ward and *All my love Lil.* And she came, just like that. Why had I never written to her before?

I saw her arrive on the thirteenth floor, press the buzzer, push her way through the heavy doors. 'All right?' she said. She rubbed hand sanitiser from the wall unit into her palms. She shook her head gently to show she understood the sadness of everything. I patted her on the back and we hugged, shy and awkward, almost kissing on the lips. Her hip bone went into my thigh at a funny angle and her cheekbone was sharp against my nose and I said, 'Ooh!' Then she smiled which was good and she laughed which was very good and we sat down together in the waiting room. I had boobs now, bosoms, breasts, whatever they are called, and she maybe felt them when we hugged, if she was interested in things like that? My development? I was two inches taller than her also. I hoped that wouldn't make me look competitive. She was wearing a striped long-sleeve T-shirt, loose dark-blue jeans, hair tied back. We chatted for about ten minutes. I could tell she was really trying. I tried to make my voice sound calm and friendly. I couldn't afford to get anything wrong. The tiredness was really getting to me. The weather we talked about. We both said what a lovely day. The pale-blue colour of the floors. No clouds.

We had not seen each other for eleven months and I knew it must have taken a lot for her to come. I offered to get her coffee, biscuits, a sandwich. The only nice thing the hospital sold to eat was apple turnovers, I told her that. They had these big crystals of sugar on the top of the pastry and they went very fast and once they're gone they're gone. 'Now I sound like a lady from the shopping channel,' I said, laughing at myself, and she smiled, unsure whether she should laugh too. I felt she was taking her lead from me. 'But it's maybe a bit early for things like that?' I added, which sounded mad, as if the hours on the clock were famously measured out in appropriate snacking rules. I knew that by being too polite you could hurt people's feelings in life; bringing serious and distant things that didn't belong on the inside of a family relationship situation. A clash. I was struggling to get my voice right. I didn't want any crying to come into it. I felt softly towards her. She was less shaky-looking than last time. She could have maybe passed for a nurse on her day off. Her eyes looked bright. Her hair in a high ponytail. Somebody's mum. She smelled like old trainers. She was very lovable.

'Sounds delicious,' she said, about the apple turnover, 'but I'm good, thanks.'

She was pretty fragile when you looked closely, the closer you got. Her skin, the surface of it, the, the texture. It wasn't convincing, maybe. Her eyes. Her breath. She was being very careful but I had the feeling there wasn't enough of anything to go round.

I wanted to show her I was well brought up. That I was sensible and calm. That the family was in pretty good shape with me in charge. I wanted to make her laugh as well. Show I had a good sense of humour. That there was quite a lot to me.

'What shall I say?' she asked me as we stood to go onto the ward.

So I told her what to say and we rehearsed it several times with me being Eleanor and her being Ruth and then the other way round. She agreed with everything, nodding and concentrating. I could tell she had proper sadness and that meant a lot to me. I took her arm and led her into the ward. I got her to wait for a minute by the nurses' station while I went across the bay to Ruth's bed.

'Hello there,' I said, very gently. 'Eleanor's here, she's come to see you to say . . . hello.'

Ruth was half asleep but her eyes opened wide. 'What, here? In the hospital?'

I nodded.

She smiled more strongly than I had seen for a long time.

OK, so I went and got Eleanor and stood by her side for a while. She did brilliantly, sitting, taking Ruth's hand, a softness in everything she said. I was so impressed. For a second I felt she was my big sister who had been away travelling or studying or, I don't know, fighting in a war. The idea that the two of us were a team. I left them together. An old lady further down the ward beckoned me over and asked me to come and sit in the chair next to her bed, so I just did that. She talked to me quickly as though she knew me very well. I didn't know who she thought I was, maybe her own daughter. 'Are you married?' she asked me at one point. I smiled mysteriously. 'Don't worry, I'm sure you'll meet someone.'

Jean arrived on the ward. When she saw Eleanor at the bedside her whole face went dark. She just stood there radiating hatred and disgust. Didn't even say hello. It was so dramatic. Her hands at the end of her sleeves rolled into fists and I thought she was going to walk right over there and have a go at Eleanor. I was shocked and my arms started shaking. What if Ruth could see? This just couldn't happen. Jesus. I jumped out of my chair, grabbed Jean's arm, asked her if I could show her something and walked her, ran her, to the other side of the bay.

'Please,' I said to her. She was panting. 'Please. For Ruth,' I said. 'Go easy on her. It's what she would want. For me. We don't have long. There can't be anything else difficult. Please. Or pretend or *something*. I am begging you. I am so grateful for everything you've done. But *please* . . .' I started to cry; stopped myself; wiped it all down my sleeve; blinked.

'OK,' she said quickly. 'Sorry,' she said a couple of times, 'my bad,' and she patted me gently on the shoulder three times then went and found Eleanor sitting at the bedside. She bent and kissed the top of her head and started chatting softly to her, through a warm smile. There were little bird-like sounds about nurses, about hospital food and the view from the window – i.e. treating Eleanor like a human being, something she obviously didn't think you had to do until it had been pointed out. I was impressed with how quickly she turned herself round, but it was all mad.

'You're a good girl, you know that?' Eleanor said to me, before she disappeared into the row of lifts.

I appreciated that, although it was what you might say to a stranger's child, a stranger's dog.

Jean had to get back to school. 'I'll pop up again at ten past four, if I may.'

I went back in, sat next to Ruth. She wasn't good at all. She couldn't take much more. Her head was shaking and her hands kept flying up, reaching for something, for someone. She tried to get out of bed, pulling on her drips and wires, but she had no strength and when I pressed her gently back down into the mattress because I was scared she would collapse on the floor, she didn't fight me.

'It's okay,' I said to her. 'It's ohhhhhh kayyyyy.' I pushed the help buzzer. I pressed it again. All my thoughts were swear words.

You were meant to be peaceful at the end but I didn't know how to get her there. 'You have had enough,' I said to her feebly and she struggled to open one eye. 'Of course you have. I am so sorry. You're doing so so well. I know you can't take it any more. We're nearly there. Nearly there now.' Was that all right to say? Could it frighten someone? Ruth nodded, weakly. She lifted her right hand and began to make a slow, jerky sideways movement as though she was trying to write me a message on the sheet, but then it dropped. I tried out a phrase in my mouth – 'I wish I could do it for you'. I would have given anything to take her place. She couldn't get there on her own. I didn't know how to make it all right. The idea I could make a mistake at this time and ruin things. That I couldn't make it better.

I took both her hands and I heard myself singing to her, very quietly, a song about fishes that we used to sing at primary school:

In middle ocean, sardines are swimming, apusski
    dusky, apusskidu.
A boat sails over, down comes a net, apusski dusky,
    apusskidu.

One wise old sardine flicks out a warning, apusski
    dusky, apusskidu.
Swift through the water, they dart away, apusski dusky,
    apusskidu.

With tails a-flashing, sardines are swimming, apusski
    dusky, apusskidu.
So full of joy that they're swimming free, apusski dusky,
    apusskidu.

Eleanor tried to pick me up from school one time. She was at the corner by the gates at four o'clock, leaning against the railings. She came up to me and she said, 'Hello, Lily Miller,' and I smiled and said, 'Hiya.' I gave her a kiss on the cheek, which was freezing, and she invited me to come home with her, said she had five cream doughnuts in her fridge today. It sounded like the first line of a children's song. I looked at her carefully and I saw that someone else, Cath or Lisa, would find her scary. I didn't, but someone else would have thought, look at her teeth and everything. Our teachers being good feminists told us that the quickest way to a meaningless life was making our appearance our main concern, but there was basic stuff you had to do. Eleanor was like a haunted house at the fair or something. Hollow bits and scabs and shadows and under it all something very sharp flickering away. It was a dark scene, her standing there asking me to go home with her. Her arms were bony and bright white but with pink and red holes that were healing over, holes that looked fresh and raw.

She saw me notice her arms and not manage myself. Quickly she rolled down her sleeves. Then she started talking about the doughnuts again, which was embarrassing, acting some idea of mothering that came from, I don't know, adverts or American TV? All I could think was that I wanted to give her a present suddenly. Or, or to say something amazing. I wished I was wearing a special piece of jewellery I could take off and put into her hands, lift up her hair and fasten round her neck. I tried out some things in my head: Look, I wish I could do it for you. I wish I could maybe, that I knew how to, that I could do something that might – do you have to—? In the end I just said I was sorry I couldn't go with her this time and I gave some excuses and she gave me a hug. At least her arms wrapped me round but they felt so stiff and strange. It made me think of a time Ruth and I were having a picnic in a church garden on one of our walks. I stopped in front of a grave, a small ancient one. There was flaky grey stone with moss in the cracks and long grasses growing all around. I started to laugh and Ruth asked me why. 'It says *Loved and Missed*,' I said.

'What's funny about that?'

'Well it kind of sounds like the person *tried* to be loving but the target moved, or the aim was wrong and the love didn't quite get through, it didn't hit home? It didn't work out for whatever reason. Or ... or ... they maybe just weren't very good at it.'

I started to cry and I turned and ran from Eleanor into the middle of a crowd of girls, who moved me forward along the street without me having to do anything. I wasn't proud of that. I liked to think I was OK with most things.

I didn't tell Ruth about Eleanor coming to the school. I should have done, I was going to, but then I thought it would be disloyal to everyone, me included. To be such a mother, to have one, to be the mother of one.

Finally the nurse came while I was standing at the bedside holding both Ruth's hands. I couldn't control it any more. I let go of Ruth for a moment and shuffled the nurse into the bathroom in the corridor, pushed the door shut, pulled the white cord for the light. She looked at me, panicky, eyes flashing wild as if I might attack. I didn't care.

'She can't take much more. Can't we do something?' I said.

'Do you mean something illegal?' Her voice was strict.

'I don't know what I'm saying.'

'Where are your parents?' the nurse said.

'You tell me.' My tone was bad. Rude. 'Sorry,' I said. 'I'm sorry.'
'Not a problem. It must be getting to you all this, I expect.'
'No, no,' I said. 'I don't mind.'

Eleanor didn't make it to the funeral. I waited till the very last minute, then I nodded to Jean, who nodded to the undertaker to close the doors. I was surprised she didn't come, but I tried not to notice because that sort of thinking doesn't do any good – and what would she have come as anyway? A ghost?

At the end I played 'Danny Boy' on my violin; the tuning wasn't great but I got through it. It was a tune Ruth loved. Easier for me than speaking anyway, we thought. Jean walked up to the front and stood with me just as I began, like my security guard, to give me strength.

I was staying at Jean's 'for a bit', but we both knew there wasn't really anywhere else for me. 'As long as you like,' she said, but we both knew I might have to stay longer than that time frame.

Jean's flat was three times the size of mine and Ruth's. It had huge windows overlooking gardens that stretched out into woods. It was modern, plumped up, comfortable, with a big skylight you could sit underneath and see stars above when it was dark. 'Rather like you've been punched in the head,' she liked to say.

Her life was more fancy than I realised: central heating, furniture spray. There was hot water at any time for as long as you liked. You could literally have three hot baths in a row. Nothing old-fashioned or crooked or broken. Her feet lived in massive fluffy pink slippers and a lot of the day was spent talking about and cooking and clearing up meals. These were enormous and often ended with an extra takeaway meal on a tray, which we carried with us to the sitting room and ate in front of the TV. Chunks of cheese and crackers, squares of chocolate, nuts and raisins. I would have been happy with just that, to be honest.

On the first Sunday she made a trifle for us with many bright layers in a tall glass bowl. Red, pink, white and yellow stripes repeating with cherries and toasted nuts on the top, to look like flowers. Little green jelly diamond leaves. I felt that we were eating her childhood.

'You're such an amazing cook,' I said.

'Well, everything Ruth made did taste strongly of wooden spoon. Sorry, sorry, sorry,' she added quickly.

There were little touches in Jean's flat I recognised from TV: gleaming white flannels in a perfect pile next to the basin and a white scented candle in a glass jar – syringa. On the back of the bathroom door there was a light-blue towelling dressing gown for me, still with its tags. Jean's standard of comfort was very high. It was one of the things she took care of deliberately, like it was work or an invalid, or some other kind of responsibility – a little kitten. To maintain it was important. Ruth and I were quite floorboard-ish in comparison. We sometimes got splinters. Jean was very lifestyle. There was always fresh orange juice and Parmesan cheese. It would never be allowed to happen that she would run out of milk or loo paper. She adored shopping. 'I am an advertiser's dream,' she said, and when we watched the adverts she cried out almost every time: 'Oh, doesn't that look wonderful?' or 'If I had some of those I'd never complain again.' Years ago she'd passed an old-fashioned chemist's with a closing-down sale and bought a whole bank of Chanel scent testers cheap. She showed me rows of small square bottles set into a black plastic rack all with little glass droppers attached to the inside of the lids. Some of the amber liquid had gone thick and sticky now. Tiny, like from a doll's house dressing table. She still got it out sometimes to play with it, she said.

I looked up syringa; it was Latin for lilac. Made me think of needles. I put the candle away.

Close up, Jean was quite ladylike. She knew the names of the women in the French bakery were Esther and Pauline.

'Have an amazing day!' they called out as we left with a bag of buns.

Jean turned back sharply. 'It's *terribly* unlikely.'

She sometimes laid the table for breakfast before she went to bed. She put out miniature boxes of cereal, hexagonal glasses for orange juice. She had baby pots of French jam with red-checked lids, guest portions that were welcoming and the opposite of welcoming because they weren't the jam of everyday. Sometimes I could see little stress bumps on her forehead from the build-up of all the things she wasn't asking. She said we ought, perhaps, to rent out Ruth's flat, as I would be glad of the money when I was at university. She was the only person I'd ever met who used the word 'perhaps' to make her words more definite.

I said, 'It's good not to make any big decisions for a year when you're bereaved, apparently.' I read that in 'Coping with a Death' at the hospital. I felt guilty flicking through the booklet when I could still hear Ruth's strong breathing, but I knew she wouldn't mind.

Jean and I were very polite – pass the salt please, hope you slept well, *lovely* shirt. I sometimes missed the Mrs Reynolds we knew from school telling us all her secrets. Her problems with her husband, sad occasions turned into mad jokes, that was her thing. The way she liked to anecdotalise her life to entertain us. His DIY phase when he was always slipping off to B&Q, or so he claimed. She laughed sharply: 'How could it take four hours to buy a medium tube of Ronseal One Coat?' The tales of her daughter, who had a 'full-blown superiority complex', in her black and cream clothing with splashes of gold. Louisa was working in banking now – 'a bloody disgrace', Jean said. 'What do you call Louisa standing on her head? An inverted snob . . . '

'I didn't know it was allowed to speak against your children,' I said to Ruth one time.

'She adores her!' Ruth was almost cross. 'It's all an act. It's just that Louisa doesn't need her and that sort of does her head in a little bit.'

Normal Jean would return when she got used to me and she relaxed. She was on her best behaviour. We both were. Her outbursts of mad honesty would probably make a comeback soon. Her sense of humour. I liked the way that although she could be quite rough with people, you always knew what she was thinking. What you see is what you get. I think that's unusual. I sometimes wondered if there were quite long stretches of life in which you couldn't afford to be yourself. In the large flat with all the luxury blue carpets and thick curtains and mountains of cushions we still had to be careful. We didn't really know what to do with ourselves. Sometimes we literally walked into each other in the corridor: Oh. Oh! Ouch! Sorry *sorry* sorry. No, no. I'm fine. All right dear? Not at all!

Jean bought me a black skirt and top the day before the funeral, quite stiff material with a silky white lining. Looked expensive, although she said not. The top had a round collar and buttons covered in the same black material. Made me look like a young widow maybe? 'You don't have to wear it,' she said. 'It was just so you wouldn't have to think.' Not thinking was a priority suddenly.

That was new in my life. That night we watched three hours of TV. Jean took her viewing very seriously. 'No no no! He's lying through his teeth,' she'd shout loudly, or 'Well, *you've* changed your tune!' I wondered if she did it when she watched alone.

'In your dreams, mate,' I called out when an old man started flirting with the young woman in the corner shop, shaking my fist feebly. Made her laugh out loud. She liked it when I showed more personality.

I woke up shivering the next morning, although the forecast said it would be nineteen degrees. My hands and feet were icy. My bones felt very stiff and sharp. I soaked in a boiling-hot bath for a while, then climbed out too quickly and fell down dizzy in a heap on the floor. I just lay there, gazing at the spotless ceiling, completely forgetting where I was. The light fitting was very shiny and modern. The luxury bath mat was foreign to me. Must have been brand new. For a second I thought it might be a hotel. What was I meant to be doing? Then I remembered. Jean's place. OK. I crept back into bed in the blue dressing gown, my arms and legs bright red.

'Don't know what's wrong with me,' I said to Jean. Ruth told me that when she was little her mother sometimes said, 'I feel as though my pilot light has gone out.' I felt like that.

'It's natural.' She smiled and brought me a tray with a bowl of hot chocolate, French style, and a warm piece of French bread and pots of butter and jam. Jean was very proud of her tray life, Ruth told me. This one had a yellow flower in a pale pink eggcup. 'Going to put a wash on, do you have anything?' she asked, perching on the edge of my bed carefully. I shook my head.

She nodded and came and sat closer to me. She took both my hands in hers over the tray. I had the feeling she wanted us to have a little cry together and we sat there for a few minutes, but nothing came. Jean thought of grief like a pet almost. A couple of times a day you had to take it out for a walk and let your thoughts wander and see if anything happened. Or sit quietly in the kitchen with some food to nibble and think about the person. Hold them close to you in your mind. In your heart. Stroke their hair. Blow on their soup for them. It's what I like to do anyway, she said. I sometimes forgot to remember that Ruth had been Jean's best friend for more than a decade. She made me up a hot-water bottle with a pink fluffy cover and I slid it into the bed. Jean's sheets and pillowcases were very soft and silky. We didn't seem to know if I was a little girl or an old lady.

Later, I wrapped the bottle in an old black lacy shawl of Jean's and took it to the funeral. 'Fantastic idea!' she said. It burned into my side, leaving a meaty red streak. I sat it on my lap in the taxi; my violin Jean held on her knee like a little child. I carried the hot-water bottle against my chest as we walked through the graveyard, which smelled of petrol and green herbs and tiny bright white star-shaped flowers. As we arrived at the chapel I passed it to her to hold for a minute while I did my shoelace. I could smell the warm rubber on my skin. With horror I saw that the pink fur wrapped in black lace in her arms looked like a dead baby. Jesus! I shoved it onto a grassy ledge next to a stone cherub for safe keeping – like Lisa says her big sister hides her trainers in the hedge outside when she goes to a party, then slips on her high heels and rings the bell. She's very cool. I carried on walking. I felt bad abandoning it, but I really did not want to upset anyone.

Nearly every teacher in the school came. It was like Founder's Day. Mrs Hadley read from the Bible. I couldn't listen. Jean and I carried the coffin in with four female undertakers. She was wearing her new black suede boots. I heard her groaning and cracking when she bent to pull them on. She'd done my hair in a French plait – 'Very dignified chief mourner,' she said, squeezing my hand. I was hoping, if Eleanor came, she might have joined in the carrying with me, but perhaps it would have been too much. 'It's not thought to be women's work,' the head man from the funeral directors said. 'But of course it is a free country and you may do as you wish.'

'We DO wish,' Jean said. 'IF we may, and we will need assistance from some of your women. Beefy ones, ideally.'

'Ah,' the man answered. And then, 'Very good.'

'An oak casket,' Jean said, 'medium-dark oak, not shiny in any way, grainy if anything, something natural she would like, the kind of wood you might use for bookshelves or for a tree. That sound right to you, Lily? Serious but not smart at all. Ivory material inside, again not shiny but high quality, sort of holy, but not bridal. Dry in texture. Woven I am thinking. Natural fibres. Heavy linen, is that something people still . . . ? Thick canvas? And I would like to pay for it if you would allow me that honour, Lily?'

I couldn't speak.

People were shocked to see women doing the carrying. Jean said it was not something she had ever seen. 'We can be proud.' The thing was unbelievably heavy. I had to concentrate very hard not just in my head but in my chest and in my elbows. 'Don't forget to breathe now,' Jean whispered. 'God, don't you just *hate* people who say that?' I giggled and she joined in. We straightened ourselves. I felt the weight of it on my shoulder afterwards for hours. When I got back to Jean's, I unbuttoned the black shirt to see if there were bruises. (There weren't.) Cath and Lisa came back to the tea afterwards. I was worried it would be awkward or boring for them, but they were great. Jean said we didn't have to join in or help or tidy up or anything. 'Perhaps just say "Thank you so much for coming" to anyone who speaks to you. Then if you smile and look down, bit of luck they'll go away.'

'OK.'

Ruth's old school friends came over in a group to say hello to me. Frances, Sarah, Christina. I wasn't certain which was which. They patted my shoulders and stroked me on my arms. 'You're an absolutely amazing young person,' one of them said. Her voice cracked on the words and I shook my head. She looked me up and down a few times and then she squeezed the top of my arm and kissed my hair just under my ear. Her face was wet and her skin looked papery, but it was very soft and warm. Her breath had red wine. Quite weird the way everyone wanted to touch you suddenly.

Cath came and rescued me. She was wearing her mum's navy Jaeger jacket, which made her look like she was going for an interview. She gave me a beautiful lace handkerchief she'd got for her first communion. 'Thank you so much!' Lisa's mum had made a special black cake with a load of rum inside. She put nuts on the top to make the letter 'R'. It was her grandma's secret recipe from Trinidad. You soaked the fruits for a whole year, apparently. Later, when most people had gone, Jean put out small dishes of nuts and raisins for us in my room, sandwich quarters, macaroons and shortbread, Cadbury's chocolate fingers, tins of Coke, cucumber and carrot sticks. 'Do your friends want alcohol?' she asked me, frowning in the face of this odd-looking kids' birthday tea. I wondered if she was following some top tips for grieving teenagers booklet. 'At five o'clock, why not offer the young people small bottles of beer?'

For days, after Ruth, Jean hummed all the time. Strange at

first, the constant low buzz which occasionally broke off and then started again, but I got used to it. It was maybe quite comforting. Now and then there was a tune I knew, but mostly it was an electric sound like a fridge or oven. Didn't know she was doing it half the time. She went quiet if I spoke to her, at least. Maybe it was a way of blocking things. A painkiller. I missed it when she stopped.

In the evenings we watched old movies on the video, Jean's green dressing gown minty fresh against her white hair. She looked like a toothbrush. She liked film noir when times were tough, she told me, you know, with women coming out on top in sharp clothing, lying through high cheekbones, emerging alluringly from train carriages in slingbacks, smoking their way out of trouble in satin blouses with bust darts, shooting people in the shoulder pads, their raised eyebrows always having the last laugh, perfect lines down the seams of their stockings. 'I love all that,' she said. *The Maltese Falcon, Double Indemnity, Sudden Fear.* I got the sense she intended these films to be an education for me, not just in the films of the past and how crime worked, and things to do with men and women, but the idea that if you were smart, like we were, you could talk your way out of almost anything. How to hold your nerve. All the ways women could triumph if they shrugged off the things that held them, held us, in check. The way the explosion of light and sound came very fast onto the screen in these films was very powerful, like bullets firing. If Jean lived in America, she would have loved all the guns.

The Sunday after the funeral we watched four films back to back in the matching red tartan pyjamas Jean bought specially for us. We ripped them out of the cellophane, size S and size XL. There was something Christmassy in the air. The great relief that the funeral was behind us, maybe. We looked like a Scottish comedy act standing next to each other, although I couldn't think of anything funny to say. Over the day we ate a whole coffee and walnut cake. It was like *we* were in a film.

Jean liked to do everything properly, to make ordinary things into an occasion. Even sitting down for a hot drink. Not to be done self-consciously, like in quotes, but each time you had ought to be a special thing, a special time, you made something out of it. An event to remember. That was life, that was living. She said it was important as you got older to take pleasure seriously. 'You must grab it by the lapels,' she said, 'hail it like a taxi.' It was one of the most important things. At any age, actually. Jean was obsessed with coffee, the drama of it and the rituals. She kept the beans in a box in the freezer, ground them down in a small green metal machine she'd bought in France. She had a special cup that she warmed with boiling water. A dreamy look came over her face. 'The baseless optimism it gives you!' Her and coffee was a love affair, she said, but *never* after three p.m. At seven fifteen she liked to have a gin and tonic, but *never* before. I liked the way all her rules gave her extra enjoyment. Usually you think of rules as taking things away. We ate the coffee cake on our laps – sticky crumbs everywhere. I found some later in my bra! There were smears of icing on the sofa arm. She didn't care. 'Let it dry and we'll just brush it off tomorrow.'

'I'm not a very good influence, am I?' I said. I felt the heaviness of the cake inside me like a brick or a baby elephant.

'You're heaven.' She was letting her guard down so I would let mine. It was working. Not a trick or anything but I knew I had to be cautious. Time was on pause now. We were between things. I kept getting caught out by the clock. Sometimes days went by and it was only forty minutes. Some of it was soft and blurry, but some of it was so sharp. I did a couple of weeks at school but I couldn't remember a single thing. In a history test I wrote the same sentence over and over. The 1870 Married Women's Property Act allowed married women to be the legal owners of the money they earned and to inherit property. The 1870 Married Women's Property Act allowed married women to be the legal owners of the money they earned and to inherit property. So strange.

'We just have to wait to get from this bit, which is terrible, to the next bit when things may start to get a little easier,' Jean said. 'That's our main job now.'

'K.'

I wrote a letter to Eleanor in fountain pen. I couldn't think what to say and I sat for a long time. Afterwards, I gave it to Jean. She put it down, waited for the clock to strike, made herself a gin and tonic, leant back into the sofa, tucked a blanket carefully round her knees. There was a small increase in the amount of tension in the room, something I had begun to measure.

> *Dear Eleanor,*
>
> *Hope you are doing OK at this time.*
>
> *Sorry not to see you at the funeral but I do understand. We tried to make things beautiful, with the music and the flowers. One lovely thing was some small cream butterflies tangled themselves up in the roses. We got everyone to sing 'SHE who would valiant be'. I played my violin. I am staying at Jean's now.*
>
> *I was wondering if you would you like to come and get whatever you want from the flat next weekend. I could meet*

you up there maybe. I know Ruth would want you to have
some special things to remember her by. I'd like it too.
     Hope you are OK.
     All my love, Lil

Jean stood up suddenly as if to say she wouldn't stand for it. Three small cushions jumped up with her – loyal little ducklings following the mama duck. She put them back carefully, setting them on their points, whacking their middles to fluff them up.

'Would you like her to come and take some stuff?' she said. 'Would you really?'

'Yeah. If she came and picked ten things or something. There must be things that have special meaning for her that she might like in her life. Things she loved and even thought of as hers, you know as a kid or . . . I mean, things that even *are* hers.'

'Perhaps you would like to remove your favourite ten things first?'

'No, I don't think so. Not too bothered about the actual stuff, for some reason.'

'That, *perhaps*, might change over time,' Jean said.

'You think?'

'In life, sometimes when we find ourselves being very generous . . .'

DO not let her drive you mad. I heard Ruth's words so often at the moment. *No doubt she'll try her best, but remember she is a good, kind, strong, hurt, sensible woman.*

'The funny thing is that things that happen in life don't really affect me all that much,' I said.

'How do you mean?'

'I'm just not one of those sort of people. I find. Who is very affected by things.'

'Oh?' Jean said.

'It's just something I've noticed,' I said. 'Here and there. I'm quite calm.'

'Oh, OK,' she said, reasonably. She sat down again, folded her hands in her lap.

I had forgotten what we were talking about already.

'Sometimes, though,' she took one of her deep breaths, which I was learning to dread, 'there are things to do with money and property and people and I know you feel strongly now, but when you are older you may well feel very differently. And my dilemma is – and it may not be right to speak of it directly to you, but I think I will anyway – is really whether to try hard to get you to see that clearly now, that you might take into account that your feelings could change, or whether that is not right.'

'*Get* me to see?'

'Make a very strong case for a different course of action that you might take.'

'Are you worried someone in the future could say you didn't do your job properly?'

'That wouldn't matter in the least, unless it was you.'

'OK.'

'So . . .'

Did she want me to sign something? Had I become one of those orphans from a book who had to be polite to the people in charge or—? Jesus. 'With stuff to do with Eleanor, the thing I have learned is whatever you do, whatever you try or don't try, or don't do, it doesn't make any difference. It's weird. But she doesn't seem to notice. Nothing ever changes. What I am saying is if I have a feeling for what will work then I sort of have to go with that, that's what I've learned. So it's not a question of choice exactly, but of having an idea about things. Having a feeling or an option, even if it's wrong or stupid, and going with that if it feels right, if it maybe makes sense? I like the idea of giving her some lovely things. It cheers me up. I need cheering up! And I've never given her anything before. Why haven't I? That isn't right. She's a vulnerable person. It's good to try new things with people. She was brilliant at the hospital, remember. She was perfect. When you . . . when she . . . '

We were silent for a moment. Jean's temples were doing that bulging rosy thing they did when she was deciding how honest to be. She could never hide what she was feeling. 'Tact rash' I had started calling it in my head, the little flashes of pink.

'I mean, what's the worst that could happen?' My voice sounded quite optimistic suddenly.

'The worst that could happen is that she picks Ruth's most valuable things, sells them right away to someone who doesn't care about them, and then, and then goes on a mad bender and overdoses.'

'I know that!'

She was trying to make sure I didn't decide anything lightly and I was trying to make it clear to her that that wasn't how I ever did anything. 'What is this *lightly*?' I wanted to say. I wanted to scream.

I wasn't sure about putting 'things to remember her by' in my letter. It could sound like I was saying she might forget Ruth – a terrible thing to write to someone's child.

Jean said it was fine. Jean said, '*Perhaps* you don't have to be that careful?'

I sent the letter, getting rid of 'to remember her by'. I added a few lines saying that Ruth's last hours had been peaceful and pain-free, which was what I'd heard other people at the hospital say about their people. I wrote that the doctor and all the nurses loved her – that *was* true. That there was calm at the very end, Jean and I holding a hand each, when she accepted it. I didn't want to make Eleanor feel bad, telling her things that could cause her regret or make her life more difficult. I sometimes felt embarrassed that my life was better than hers. If I said please take what you want, it was a chance to make things up to her. To show I knew the things that made her life hard I didn't have inside me and that was my privilege.

In the days and weeks after Ruth died I thought about Eleanor all the time. Had I stolen from her? In the letter I suggested she came to the flat the following Sunday afternoon. I'll leave the key under the stone behind the bins, I wrote. Said I would drop in at four-ish in case she needed a hand, as if we were always arranging to meet here and there when the fact was this wasn't something we had ever done apart from that one time at the hospital. That had gone well. An American TV psychologist I liked said the best indicator of future behaviour was past behaviour. I felt excited. I would be returning to her something she already owned. Not compensation exactly but showing I knew how lucky I had been and what was right.

The legal facts were Ruth left everything to me. Jean read me the will, sitting at her dressing table with all the perfume bottles and the mirror. Eleanor's flat could not be sold unless Jean, me and Eleanor all gave our permission. 'That's very good,' Jean said. 'That was my doing.'

I wanted Eleanor to have anything she wanted. We would divide things between us, in fairness. I have never thought she was a bad mother. I read this book in the spring about estranged families that made me realise mothering hadn't really given her a chance. For example, I would not say I was a bad driver because I hadn't ever had a lesson. So who's to say? I might be brilliant.

Jean tried once more to talk me out of it. 'It doesn't feel right,' she said quietly.

'What are you worried about?'

'My worry is she could come with a lorry and take every single thing. Sit down a minute.' She told me a story from a novel she liked where exactly this happened. The young man had told his widowed mother she could take a handful of things, a 'very good handful from the house that now was his, anything she fancied before he moved in with his new wife, and she had hired many vans and many men and taken everything of interest or value or beauty. Hundreds and hundreds of items, almost everything, all packed up and transported across the country so that the house, shorn of its wonders, nude and hollow, could no longer function as a home. She hated the new wife, you see,' Jean added. 'Knew she wouldn't appreciate the lovely things. The wife was rather a brute, truth be told.'

'You can't believe everything you read in books, Jean!' I thought that was witty. I gave her elbow a little shove.

'I mean, how would you feel if she emptied the flat?'

I thought about it for a second. 'I would be honoured.'

She groaned and the colour went out of her face, which was dramatic as she always wore a lot of blusher and now she looked like a frightened clown.

'The only thing I really want is the red colander. It sort of *is* Ruth.'

'Well at the very least take that.'

'I already have.' I went and fetched it from under my bed and put it on my head. 'Do you like my new hat?' I said. 'It's breathable.' She started to laugh.

'Aren't we getting on well, though?' she said.

Jean's encouragement of me that week was crazy. She stirred it into stews. She baked it into cakes. You can be *anything you want to be*, you can do *whatever you like*, and there is nothing, *nothing* you cannot have; she recited these sorts of things at the bus stop, or while we were doing our teeth. We ate custard creams at bedtime and did our teeth again and then had a couple more. 'What the fuck,' Jean said. There was never any 'considering' in Jean's encouragement of me, no 'after what you've gone through/been through/come through' – which I appreciated. Sometimes I heard in her bright enthusiasm 'you can be anything *I* want', but that might have been unfair. She was like a TV fitness guru with her catchphrases every morning. And her encouragement was so random: 'Good job!' just for getting out of bed and getting dressed, or spreading apricot jam on my toast. 'Classy of you not to go for the strawberry.' So the jam was like a character test? It was quite an exhausting way to live, Jean trying to fill me up with confidence all day long, all night, wanting the best for me. Did she think if we felt bad we were failing? One evening I caught her looking at me while we were watching TV with an expression of soft amazement and I felt certain she preferred me to her own child.

Was I someone people came to for a second chance?

On Saturday morning she was hovering again. 'Can I ask you something absolutely excruciating and ask in advance that you forgive me?'

'Um, what? Yeah, I suppose.'

'Have people ever talked to you much about the facts of life, as they were called in 1066. Sex and so on. Relationships. Love. Orgasms. Contraception. Who takes the bins out, that order of things?'

'Er, yes, I think I am ... all good.'

'Contraception particularly, I suppose, is of the—'

'Thing is, if my family had been good at contraception, I wouldn't be here.'

'Ah. Fair enough.'

A couple of weeks before Ruth died, Jean picked out four girls in my year and told us, crossly, that after we did our GCSEs next summer we must set our minds on Oxford. She shooed us into her form room at lunchtime. Be really *stupid* not to. She spat out 'stupid' like a curse. It was our duty. 'You are strong, clever and able. These are talents that carry with them responsibility.' There was definitely threat in her voice. She was almost scowling. 'D'you understand?' (She had maybe been watching too many gang-ster movies.) Jean had such a fear of sounding sentimental that sometimes when she praised you it felt like she was telling you off. Education, to her, was a bit like love but with all the emotion taken out of it. Emotion had betrayed her in her life in a variety of ways, she said.

At school, people tiptoed round me. The girls in my year were very young for their age. One afternoon I read a story in the local paper about a postwoman who had been jailed for seven-teen months for taking all the mail back to her flat in Somers Town. There was a photo of where she lived, with a sea of letters, 43,000 assorted envelopes and packets, white and brown, all over the floor. At the edge of the photograph there was an old-fashioned gas cooker and an unmade bed and in the middle a

white plastic garden-type chair had fallen down on its back and
lay like a drunk animal on top of all the post. Next morning we
were sitting in the classroom at break. I wanted to talk about the
postwoman's state of mind. Some girls were reading lines to each
other from a play – *Lysistrata*, where the women of Greece went
on a sex strike in order to get the men to end the war – that was
having auditions later in the week. I thought the postwoman
story showed some painful need on the woman's behalf, a mad
fantasy brought on by loneliness that all the letters were for
her. That she wanted popularity or control. Communication,
answers, cheques, attention, love, birthday cards, money-off
coupons. More life in her life. I had the feeling in the classroom
no one was really listening to my thoughts on her psychology.
'What do you think it all means?' I asked.

'It means she knew fuck all about doing her job.'

That was disappointing.

Ruth told me her mother hated getting letters because she
couldn't imagine news that wasn't bad. Jean said the damage war
did was beyond a modern person's imagining.

I looked up which Oxford college had the most people from
comprehensives. I pored over the angular 1960s building, dark
glass and brick and concrete, bleak in appearance but with a water
garden running alongside filled with grasses and reeds and actual
lily pads. There were boxy glass rooms stacked on top of each
other, shimmering green from the reflected garden light. Serious,
Ruth would have said, and democratic, professional. I didn't know
then that a little further up the hill there were pale golden Disney
buildings from the thirteenth century with gargoyles and turrets
and rose gardens and girls with long hair in floaty dresses sitting
in boats with bottles of champagne and straw hats. I didn't need

to know. It would not have made a difference. That kind of thing embarrassed me.

Jean's house was so hot you could wander about all day in your underwear – not that we did. She told me she was freezing her entire childhood and when she first got her hands on some cash she vowed she would NEVER be cold again. She was proud of her ferocious heating. She said, 'Even being without things I really don't want can make me feel deprived. If I'm too hot at night it's impossible for me to throw the covers off. It would be a grave act of disloyalty to my shivering self. Too much of something feels like defiance. It's victory over adversity. I operate as a camel half the time. It's why I'm fat, I suppose. And I don't hate waste either. It feels luxurious. Unfashionable, I know.' She often talked about her childhood. She said that everything she did in the present was a reaction to its deprivations. I think it was her way of encouraging me to speak about my life.

I already knew more about her early years than I did about Ruth's. Jean's mother had died when she was fourteen and she didn't tell anyone at school. 'I didn't want the girls to have any-thing on me, to be caught on the back foot. Know what I mean? I got by all right. Came home from school every day, made myself a hot-water bottle, stuck it up my jumper, worked my way through half a loaf spread with my mother's jam. She left jars and jars. I was eating it for years. That and the telly meant I was never alone.' Then a few seconds later: 'I was quite proud in some ways. It would have been excruciating in the playground having people define you by life events you hadn't chosen. That didn't seem to have much to do with who you were in yourself.'

I nodded to show I had received what she said.

Sunday came and Jean brought me tea and toast in the morning, perching on the edge of the bed as she liked to. I sometimes felt she wished she could climb in. She wanted to discuss the contents of the flat again, but I shut it down. I wrapped the toast in loo roll, put it in an envelope, stuffed it deep into the kitchen bin. It felt like protecting my privacy. At lunchtime I went for a long walk. She will try to drive you mad, Ruth said, but remember she is a *good, kind, strong, hurt, sensible woman*. Yeah, yeah, I thought, and then: I know, maybe fresh air will help me. Ruth was very big on fresh air; the way walking often helped things fall into place. That it calmed you. I walked all the way to Regent's Park. I threw some of the stale funeral cakes at the ducks and swans but I didn't stay long. I preferred streets and traffic and buses and shops to willow trees, goslings, decorated bridges, rowing boats, which seemed to me the opposite of reality. They had all lost their grip. I bought a toffee ice cream from Baskin Robbins but it tasted tragic so I threw it away. I hadn't been able to eat much lately. Jean put out dishes of cheese chunks and cucumber and apple slices and wholewheat crackers and said if I ate them all it would be enough, so I just did that. I sat down on the pavement outside the entrance to Baker Street station, next to the lost property office. It was very bright and the streets were busy and noisy with people living their lives.

I started to cry for Ruth. I cried for her high standards, for the dignified way she carried herself as though the difficulties of life were in some way her great honour. I cried for her faith in herself. I cried for the fact that there was nothing about her that was in the slightest way second best. I cried because she was so calm and together. I cried because I couldn't believe I would never see her again. I cried because the tips of her fingers always looked so red and cold peeping out of her fingerless gloves, which she liked because full gloves made her claustrophobic. I cried because she had gone out of her way to make me feel I was precious and valuable. I cried because I never once saw her buy herself anything nice. I cried for the pain she carried in her heart, her lack of power and control over her life a sort of prison at times, and never asking for help or complaining. The good mood she put on like a uniform every morning. Her smile. That sense we had that we understood each other, without having to say anything, that we knew how to be careful, not anxious careful, just full of care, full of caring. That the things that made us sad also made us strong, were our power.

I must have closed my eyes, because when I looked at my watch it was ten past four and I panicked. I ran for a bit then I jumped on a bus at the lights. I hoped Eleanor wouldn't mind me being late. The idea she could think I didn't care was horrific.

I hadn't been back into the flat since the funeral. I was nervous. I didn't even know what to hope. I was worried about Eleanor's feelings, and Jean I had been harsh with, I saw that now. Piles and piles of mistakes everywhere. I should have tried to get them back together long before the end. Why didn't I? Even the postwoman who took the letters back to her flat to keep her company – I felt her laughing at me. And what if Eleanor did take everything? My stomach was heaving. I felt the sharpness of all the acid brewing up inside me; knots of panic. Then I remembered there were still two bottles of Ruth's morphine at the flat, 10mg/5ml, one full, one three quarters ... JESUS. I stopped next to a litter bin and was sick – three small, clear mouthfuls – wiped my mouth on my sleeve. How could I be so dangerous?

I went to a meeting for families, a while ago. I got the 29 to the West End, snuck in the back, didn't tell anyone. A woman said when her son tried heroin for the first time he felt a great rush of what he described to her as 'peace and protection'. She had not been expecting that. That drugs could give him a feeling of health and of safety. She told him that when she had been pregnant with him she had been prescribed morphine for her cancer, so he recognised the, not the flavour of it, I can't remember the word she used. The feel of it, the lull of it, the cure of it. He felt his search for happiness was over, she said. That was how strong his attachment was. What I was dealing with. He said it felt like love.

The room went completely quiet and then a woman in a green shirt suddenly shot out of her seat and shouted, 'Yeah, but he would say that, wouldn't he? Of course he'd make it your fault – the cunt – that's what they do! You're not meant to believe them.' Someone else started talking wildly and tried to sit the woman down. A fight broke out. The man in charge stood up on his chair and held his arms out: 'Hey hey hey,' he boomed. 'Kindly remember that in these rooms we discourage all cross-talk and interrupting.' Chairs scraped back and there was a lot of gasping and tutting. I left in a daze. Walked all the way home. Stopped at the McDonald's near Warren Street and bought a cheeseburger, swallowed it down in half a minute. Warm soft bread, salt, sugar, pickle, grease. I kept on walking.

Eleanor would take nothing from the flat but those brown bottles. I knew it now. My eyes filled, my head was banging against its walls. I saw her and me sitting at the kitchen table spooning morphine into each other, like a tea party, jellies in paper cases. One for mummy, one for baby. I should have let Jean come. Jean was so straightforward and I sometimes saw it as a lack of ideas, but it was pure strength. I pictured Eleanor lying completely still. Maybe a neighbour would help me get her out of there, force the lock on the bathroom door, bundle her into an ambulance. Walk her round the room until she woke, until the ambulance came, feet dangling, matchstick jelly legs.

I ordered a naloxone kit with my Christmas money once. It had a 'pre-filled syringe for reversing opiate overdose'. Thought we should keep one in the flat maybe. Pop it under the bed. Just in case. I didn't say anything about it to Ruth. It was easy to use, apparently. They included the needle and everything you needed. *Anyone can administer naloxone in an emergency to someone they believe may have overdosed.* But the thing never came. The company was a trick maybe? Sixteen quid down the drain. Not the end of the world. Maybe I was relieved?

In an emergency, would I have the strength to carry her down the stairs into the street? There wasn't much to her. Maybe the new woman in the basement flat would help. It started to rain; the raindrops streaking warm and dirty on my skin. If only she was waiting for me on the corner now. Someone like Ruth. Ruth! I called out into the afternoon air. Ruth! It was like another Greek play suddenly. Tell me, did you mean to kill your mother by mistake?

I ran up our street, slithering through rotted blossom, sweat trickling between my shoulder blades, the facts of my life accelerating without me. There were no lights on in our flat that I could see, but then it wasn't dark. There was an old car I didn't recognise outside, the exhaust pipe dangling, and in the hallway someone had dumped a shiny leather coat, but I was pretty sure it was a man's. It was very quiet everywhere. I raced up the stairs, damp footprints on the carpet, digging the key into my palm until it hurt. The door I could barely open because of all the letters piled up. Mostly bills, but some of the envelopes were addressed to me. I pushed them out of the way with my foot, squeezed through the opening into the hall. *Dear Lily, We were so shocked and sorry to hear the very sad news.*

Ruth was everywhere: the smell of onions frying and the French carnation soap she liked for Christmas and all the stale medicines and the knitting wool and seven decades' worth of books, thousands of paragraphs and chapters and sentences with tiny clever pencil markings in the margin – *his most Miltonian sonnet surely* and *cf. A. E. Housman.* Above all in the air there was her pride. It rushed at me. I went into the bathroom, saw the two bottles of Oramorph in the cupboard where they belonged. I lifted them and they felt full in my hands. I peered into the bedroom, sat on the edge of the bed, neatly made as we'd left it, the maroon quilted cover with its dull shine dramatic-looking against the white sheet neatly folded. A green jug of dried flowers and her book wedged open on the bedside table – *Bonjour Tristesse.* When we started on it I thought, what if this isn't good enough, not to end with? That it wasn't a great work. I said this to Jean and she was crisp. 'Sometimes in life,' she said, 'a really quite good book is what you need more than an excellent one.' That scared me. It was so un-Jean. Perhaps it *was* meant to be very good, I didn't know what I was talking about. The cover was quite cheap-looking, with a half-naked girl. I should have maybe said something. Different rules at the end of life, was it? It would have taken her back to when she was young, Jean explained later on.

There was a thin layer of dust on everything, a frame with a picture of me as a baby with these little curls, so cute; a tortoiseshell comb that still had one grey-brown hair. I put the hair and the comb into an envelope, slipped it in my bag with the photo of me in the frame to keep it company. I laid my cheek on the pillowcase and breathed her in.

At the end, I promised Ruth everything. I said I'd get Eleanor well. Said I had a plan that couldn't fail. Weak as she was, she gave me a doubtful look. You will have your work cut out. We both knew there was nothing better I could give her. It was the best thing I had. Then, 'Oxford?' she mouthed. She was always ambitious for me. I'm not saying it was bad, but it was funny to be brought up to think the world was mine because of what the people before me had lost.

'Lovely girl.' She struggled to make the words. She was sleeping gently. I touched her hair with my crooked little finger.

'Good night, angel.'

She looked at me carefully. 'Not yet!'

I must remember to crack jokes in my last hours.

A sound came from behind me and I jumped up, but there wasn't anyone. A mouse maybe? We sometimes had one, pinkish and scuttling, quite mad in her character – Flora was her name. I went into the kitchen; felt the kettle, which was cold. The front room was lifeless except for a brown moth flapping round the inside of the lampshade. Was that what I heard? The curtains were thin against the windows; I used to think of them as light but I saw now they were not good quality – compared to Jean's. Nothing was missing. I sat down on the sofa, roughly banging my shin on the corner of the table. Of my mother there was no sign. Business as usual, the invisible woman.

I hardened myself deliberately. I felt myself change in that minute. I saw my fingers stiffening, caught a different rhythm in my breaths. It was rage, I suppose. Terrible in life when you wanted to give everything and there wasn't anyone willing to receive you. Some people believed that if your mother wasn't all that bothered about you she must know more than anyone what you were really like, deep down, because she sort of invented you so, so there had to be something really wrong with you then. I didn't think that way myself. But I had read it was important to allow all the feelings in so they had no power over you and you could be set free. Not to hold back on anything because it was too bad to say. To have a mother who wasn't maternal.

I sat there as it got dark just rocking myself backward and forward on our sofa. Ruth's old cardigan was still draped over the chair and I felt the dry wool. Held it up to my nose. I had the sense that I was never again going to feel what I was feeling. That I wouldn't allow it because it was too painful. The moment was sharp, the empty room throbbing, the darkness closing its edges around me. I draped the cardigan over my shoulder, put my arms in the sleeves.

Quite a while later I saw the street lights coming on and then I heard Jean's voice calling from the landing, soft knocking on the door.

'Lily, Lily, are you there, dear? Can you hear me? May I come in, please? Are you OK? I've got us coffees. I've got sandwiches and cake. I've got the number for a minicab.'

I went to the door, my legs buckling beneath me, and there was Jean with her intelligent, curious face and bright hair, her arms spread out as though she was an aeroplane or a scarecrow or Jesus Christ up on his cross, and my strength went and I sagged against her chest.

'Fucking hell, Jean.'

'I know.'

We stood in silence for a bit with Jean holding me up, and then she said, 'Tell me what you're thinking,' and I did.

'This doesn't make sense. It's not what I was ready for. I always thought it would be my mum. That we'd get a bad phone call in the middle of the night. I couldn't stand the sound of the phone. Once on my birthday there was a bad phone call early, I think she must have overdosed, and we just went ahead with the party. But then later I heard you tell Ruth they let her go so I knew she was alive. Or if I saw a policeman in the street I hid because I thought he was going to have bad news for me because on TV policemen always come to the house. And I didn't like the news being on in case they said she had died. I know that doesn't make sense because she wasn't famous or anything. But the people we love are always famous in our heads. To children. Also, that she would die without any warning, without saying goodbye, that frightened me. If I hadn't seen her for a long time or if she died all on her own. That would be unbearable. With no one to help her. So I tried to think it might happen at any moment, so that there could already be a sort of warning, to protect myself. I didn't want to get caught out. That I saw it coming. I just didn't think Ruth would go first. That was never a possibility. She was so strong. Permanent. It's just so wrong when parents die before their children.'

Jean opened her mouth and closed it again and her lips settled into a look of great concern. I didn't need that, but you couldn't tell people what you felt and insist they didn't react. You could when you were older maybe, if you knew someone really well. Like if you'd been married for fifty years or something, to someone really nice, then they would just know how you liked them to behave. When to be careful, when to challenge, how seriously to take you. You'd have it prearranged. Jokes to calm you down. Times when a joke wouldn't help at all.

'I can't think of the words. I'm sorry,' I said. Jean hated that sort of talk. At school she had been known to put a green line through a paragraph and write *waffle waffle waff waff*. 'There's just one of me now,' I said, 'isn't there? Floating about without anything to hang onto, without anything to hold me down. Isn't that . . . I don't really know what to . . . Sorry,' I said. 'Sorry.'

'No. What you say is important.'

'I'm like a single-person family, aren't I?'

She shook her head. 'I am so sorry about that,' she said. I was glad she didn't contradict me. 'I hope I can be sort of like family to you, the good of family with none of the bad. If that's possible. That is what I would like, if you could stand it. I would never presume anything.'

'Thanks.'

'I've driven people mad all my life, and I really wouldn't want to add another name to the list of casualties.' She smiled.

I didn't know how to answer. 'OK?' I said. My voice was cautious.

She laughed. 'And you made Ruth so happy.'

'Did I?'

'The difference was obvious to everyone who knew her. She was completely transformed after you came into her life.'

That was a bit more than I could take.

Finally: 'Let's get you home,' she said.

'This is my home.'

Jean closed her eyes for a second. I had the sense of a tiny woman walking round and round an enormous building looking for doors. 'I mean, would you like us to come and live here?'

I shook my head. 'No, that wouldn't be right, it's not, you couldn't be expected to, after everything. And your place is so you.'

'I would. Happily, not happily, because obviously this whole thing is sadder than fuck, but you know what I'm saying.'

'Yeah.'

'Why don't you think about it?'

'K.'

'In other news,' she said carefully, 'I've got something to tell you. It's unexpected and the timing isn't perfect, but . . . well, Louisa's eldest, Izzy, is going to have a baby. A little girl.'

'What? How old is she?'

'She's your age. Fifteen.'

'Jesus!'

'I know.'

'OK, so, well that's . . . How do you feel?'

'Well, a whole new female person is always good news, is what I said to Louisa. And I do think I shall be a rather *great* grandmother.'

'And is the dad . . . ?'

'Well I did ask about him and she said to me, "Nana, you know boys? Well, I think they just aren't quite fully *people* in the way that girls are?"'

I started to giggle although I was crying as well. 'You must have been proud.'

Jean blew me a kiss. 'Of course Louisa's furious, but she seems to want me involved.'

'Maybe I could help you?'

'That would be brilliant actually. Do you like babies? They're not everyone's cup of tea by any means.'

I blinked. 'I don't really know any. But people do go on about how sweet they are and everything.'

'They can be, certainly. I mean, they're like people. Some of them are magnificent creatures and others scrape the barrel rather. Blobby and sort of mind-numbing. Perhaps we'll be in luck with this one. Fingers crossed in any case.'

'Jean!'

She gathered up my bag and put it over her shoulder, swivelled my empty coffee cup inside hers. She picked up my hand, like a Disney prince to a maiden, and gave it a kiss. Courtly love, that was what it was called – with dragons and lace-collared knights. Mrs Reynolds taught us that in Year 10. 'NOT to be confused with Courtney Love,' she said. '*Quite* different.' She held out the arms of my jacket for me and I slipped it on.

And going down the stairs, I stopped for a moment: 'Do you know things, Jean, that I don't?'

She turned to face me. 'About your life, do you mean?'

'Yeah.'

She came up to my step and swatted me lightly on the arm.

'One or two, one or two.'

Credits

Epigraph	Stevie Smith, 'I Forgive You', from *The Collected Poems and Drawings of Stevie Smith* (London: Faber and Faber, 2015). Reproduced by permission of Faber and Faber Ltd
26	Howard A. Walter, 'I Would Be True' (1906)
35	Elizabeth David, *French Provincial Cooking* (London: Michael Joseph, 1960)
165	'Apusski Dusky' (traditional Swedish song)

I am also grateful to Sarah Hart for *A Mother Apart.*

Susie Boyt is the author of seven novels and the memoir *My Judy Garland Life*, which was short-listed for the PEN Ackerley Prize, staged at the Nottingham Playhouse, and serialized on BBC Radio 4. She has written about art, life, and fashion for the *Financial Times* for many years and recently edited *The Turn of the Screw and Other Ghost Stories* by Henry James. She is also a director at the Hampstead Theatre. She lives in London with her family.